M.I.A.

A Story Inspired by True Events

Bogdan Sopterean

• Chicago •

M.I.A.

A Story Inspired by True Events

Bogdan Sopterean

Joshua Tree Publishing

JoshuaTreePublishing.com

13-Digit ISBN: 978-1-956823-62-2

Cover Image Credit: Bogdan Sopterean

Disclaimer:

This is a work of fiction, inspired by true events. Names, characters, places, and incidents are the product of the author's imagination or have been used fictitiously. Any resemblance to actual persons, living or dead, events, locales or organizations is entirely coincidental. The content presented herein is based on the author's perspective and interpretation of the subject matter. Neither the publisher nor the author shall be held responsible for any consequences arising from the opinions or interpretations expressed within this book.

Printed in the United States of America

Dedication

To my wonderful Grand Aunt Maria.

I am very blessed that I had you in my life from the first day I was born. You welcomed me into your home with your arms wide open, you taught me the power of love, the power of prayer, and the power of kindness. I never saw you take a step back when someone was in need of your help. Moreover, you went above and beyond to make sure that everyone was good.

You were, you are, and you always will be one of the biggest and strongest stones in the foundation of my life.

I love you and thank you again for everything that you have done for me.

God rest your soul in peace.

The Year Was 1949

At the age of thirty-two, Maria just purchased her first three-bedroom apartment in the city of Cluj-Napoca, commonly known as Cluj, which is the second most populous city in Romania after the national capital, Bucharest.

Geographically speaking, it is roughly equidistant from Bucharest (201 miles), Budapest (218 miles), and Belgrade (200 miles), and the city is considered the unofficial capital of the historical province of Transylvania.

Given that Maria's apartment could easily accommodate another family, Maria gladly offered her brother Patrick and his family the opportunity to move in with her. Patrick and his wife, Ana, had a three-year-old daughter and another child on the way, and they were living in a small village two hours outside the city, requiring Patrick to commute by bus every day to work.

Therefore, the opportunity for an easier life was too good to refuse. As a result, with only a few weeks left before Patrick's wife gave birth to their baby boy, they eagerly moved into Maria's apartment.

However, their relocation was not only a positive change for them. It was also a positive change for Maria, as she recalled:

"I began to be a vital part of their family from the day their baby boy was born, and that made me feel happy and alive again. My brother Patrick and his wife, Ana, even let me choose a name for their son. So I named him Octavian, and I began treating him like he was my own son from the very first second I held him in my arms."

Maria loved taking care of Octavian any chance she could get, yet she was needed the most in raising Octavian from the moment Ana reached the end of her maternity leave and had to return to her job at the candy factory. But since Maria had already offered Patrick's family her apartment as their new home in the city, Patrick and Ana did not want to appear like they were taking advantage of Maria's kindness when she offered to take care of their son during the day. So they decided to take their son to the same childcare where their daughter happily spent the day.

Nonetheless, the moment Octavian had to be dropped off on his first day of childcare, he started to shed tears and kindly asked his aunt to go back home with her.

Maria felt heartbroken to watch the sadness in Octavian's eyes when she left him there. Yet she kept trying to follow the wishes of Octavian's parents and continued to drop him off at the childcare for the rest of the week. But then, once she and Octavian shared how they felt with Patrick and Ana, Maria's kind offer to take care of their son while they went to work was kindly accepted. From that moment, Maria and Octavian became joined at the hip, and their days spent together blessed Octavian with many different experiences.

One day, he would be walking with his aunt in the park; the next day, he would be in the city learning about the surroundings and the city's history from his aunt. The following day, he would find himself by the edge of the forest nearby their apartment, having a delicious picnic that his aunt prepared for them. And any other day, perhaps he would find himself sitting by the river near their church, just enjoying nature.

However, each Sunday, they would follow a typical routine. First thing in the morning, Maria would take Octavian to church. Then, after they returned home from church, they would eat lunch with the entire family before Maria would take Octavian to her favorite place, the theater, where she would always place him in the balcony seats on the first level, on the side of the stage that made him feel as if he was part of the play. Thus, the theater quickly became one of Octavian's favorite places to be as well.

All that mattered to Maria was to keep Octavian happy, and slowly, over the years, the bond that existed between them became stronger and deeper. Maria's kindness and constant companionship proved to be even more than an aunt-nephew relationship. Maria became like a second mother to Octavian, whose presence always soothed him in any circumstance. Because of that, it became harder for Octavian to leave her during summer vacation when he and his sister, Felicia, had to visit their grandparents in the village again for two months at a time.

The reason Patrick and Ana sent Octavian and Felicia to their grandparents was to give their children a taste of the farm life they had experienced growing up. They wanted them to enjoy fun activities like chasing chickens through the yard and the messy job of feeding pigs, which was as entertaining as learning how to brush and pet horses and sheep. On top of that, the fruit at the end of an adventurous tree climb was always rewarding.

Every single thing Octavian and his sister did at their grandparents' farm was totally different from their life experience in the city, but there wasn't anything to dislike about the farm life.

However, the year Octavian turned six years old, he knew he would start first grade soon after returning home from the farm. So that year, he tried to convince his parents to let him stay at home to spend more time with his aunt. Despite his attempt, Octavian still found himself at the farm, where he began counting down the days until his parents would pick him up as promised on the Sunday before school started.

Typically, Patrick and Ana would arrive in the morning around 7:00 a.m. so they could have plenty of time to take Octavian back to the city for his Sunday routine with Maria. But that year, the day he was supposed to be picked up to return to the city, his parents were late.

It was already 8:45 a.m., and Octavian was still impatiently waiting on the bench in front of his grandparents' house for his parents to arrive. Half an hour later, they still weren't there, and as the minutes passed, Octavian became more and more upset. He had no choice but to wait restlessly on the bench, looking as far as his eyes could see, hoping to see his parents' car appear in the distance.

Time kept passing, and because there wasn't any trace of his parents, Octavian couldn't look away from the road.

Suddenly, he began to shout happily, "I see them! They're finally here!" and ran toward the house to grab his backpack.

However, by the time Octavian's parents said goodbye to his grandparents and got into the car to leave, it was already 10:30 a.m. Even though they realized it would be impossible to get back home before noon, meaning Octavian would probably miss the entire mass, which was part of his long-awaited Sunday routine with his aunt, Patrick still wanted to drive directly to the church to see if they could still find Maria there. After all, a promise was still a promise.

People were already leaving the church as soon as they arrived, and since Maria usually stayed until the end, Octavian decided to hide just outside the open doors to surprise her. He waited eagerly behind the door for a few minutes, but when there was still no sign of his aunt, he peeked into the church to see if he could see her. Suddenly, he felt a hand on his shoulder.

"Octavian, is that you?"

That startled him, but as soon as he turned around, he saw that it was Mrs. Joanna, one of Maria's good friends.

"I haven't seen you for a while. What are you doing here, hiding behind the door?" asked Mrs. Joanna.

"Hello, Mrs. Joanna. I am waiting for my aunt. I am trying to surprise her. Have you seen her?" Octavian asked curiously.

"Yes, I saw her. But she left about twenty minutes ago before mass was over. She didn't look well, but when I asked her if she was all right, she told me that she was fine and that she was going by the river."

As soon as Octavian heard Mrs. Joanna say his aunt went to the river, he knew exactly where she would be, so he started running as fast as his legs could carry him toward his aunt.

During the mass, Maria started to feel dizzy and nauseous, and her vision became blurry. She didn't know what was happening to her or how to react, so she decided to go outside for some fresh air and take a nice walk along the Little Somes River. Walking along the river always made Maria feel peaceful because of its calm surroundings. The sound of the wind and the water splashing over the rocks, blended with the music made by tiny musicians dressed in colorful feathers, always reminded her of a soothing symphony.

But then, just when Maria believed she was feeling better, she suddenly got struck with a severe headache that dropped her to the ground, leaving her lying there alone while staring at the blue sky, frozen in fear.

Then she heard a voice . . .

Chapter One

The Beginning

World War I
August 12, 1917

It was ironic to be born at the same time the world was taking lives through a heartless war, but August 12, 1917, was the day Maria was ready to enter the light of our world. That day, Maria's mother, Katrina, was not only fighting the pain of labor but also the fear of staying alive as their village was under an aerial attack, with multiple bombs being dropped everywhere.

"Come on! Let's go! We can't stay here, Katrina. The house will fall apart any second. We have to get out right away!" screamed Elisabeth desperately to her sister, Katrina, who was lying on the floor, unable to handle the pain from the contractions.

"I can't get up, Elisabeth! I don't have any strength to move. Just go! Go! Save yourself!" cried Katrina as her eyes flooded with tears.

Elisabeth and Katrina needed to leave the house quickly. Small chunks of the ceiling started to crumble around them, and the structure of the house showed its weakness through the many cracks that had appeared on every wall.

It was only a matter of time until they would be trapped inside the house, joining the number of people already taken away by the heartless war.

"I'm not going anywhere without you! We must leave my house right away, even if I have to carry you, Katrina! Please! We have to go! We need to get to the church. We will be safe there," responded Elisabeth. With a final effort, she helped her sister, Katrina, stand up and hastily dragged her out of the house.

The church was about two miles away, right outside of their village, near the forest, and it was the only place Elisabeth could have thought of going for shelter and hopefully getting some help for her sister to give birth.

However, to get to the church, Katrina and her sister, Elisabeth, needed to walk through the darkness of the night and pass through several obstacles. The most threatening obstacle was the deadly rain of artillery shells falling from the sky, silencing the screams of terror and leaving many people lifeless on the blood-soaked ground. Under this deadly rain of artillery shells, Katrina and Elisabeth could not stop walking until they reached the church.

They began to walk as fast as they could, but Katrina's energy was swiftly fading, and her legs were becoming too weak to support her own weight. But she needed to keep going.

Elisabeth, whose strength was also slowly fading, began to struggle to hold her sister up. Even though they both needed to stop and catch their breath, they knew they needed to keep moving. Yet, when Katrina caught a glimpse of the church, her legs gave out, and she collapsed to her knees, pulling her sister down to the ground with her.

Elisabeth, nearly unable to stand back up, clumsily grabbed at Katrina to pull her back to her feet, but she could barely stand herself.

"I am going to bring someone who can help us," Elisabeth said as she clutched Katrina's hand. Then she turned around and began walking as fast as she could toward the church. "Please, someone help me!" Elisabeth yelled as she got closer to the church.

No one from the church could hear her yelling since the sounds of the war easily drowned out her voice. But as soon as she got in front of the closed doors of the church, she started pounding and kicking on them with all the strength that she had left.

"Please open the doors! I need help! Someone, please open the doors!" Elisabeth yelled as loud as she could.

Luckily, a man's voice could be heard from inside.

"Let's open the doors!" said the man.

Soon, the doors opened, and a young couple hurried outside to help Elisabeth while an elderly man who appeared to be the priest of the church stood in front of the doors, holding a lit oil lamp in his hands.

"My sister is in labor, and she needs your help!" exclaimed Elisabeth as she pointed toward her sister, who was lying on the ground not far away.

While the woman remained with Elisabeth, the young man ran toward Katrina and quickly picked her up in his arms, walking back to the church as fast as he could.

As soon as the old man saw Katrina, he recognized her right away.

"Let's take her into the basement right away!" he shouted, locking the doors behind them.

"I'll put some water on to heat up, and I'll bring some clean sheets," continued an elderly woman who became visible as she lit up another oil lamp near the stairs leading into the basement.

About forty-five minutes had passed before Katrina delivered the baby, and everyone standing around listened with joy to the loud sound of the baby crying, which momentarily interrupted the sound of artillery fire from outside.

The priest cut the baby's umbilical cord while Elisabeth held the baby. Then, as she handed the baby to her sister, she said, "Katrina, you have a beautiful baby girl."

Katrina's eyes began to flood with tears of joy as she held her baby, who gazed into her eyes. But then, her joy quickly faded to tears of sorrow because her husband was unable to be with them.

"I wish Daniel could be here right now. I miss him so much. It isn't fair!" Katrina said to her sister, thinking of her husband.

"Everything is going to be all right. At least we have each other for now. Just try to relax and get some rest. I'll be right here next to you," Elisabeth said, trying to put her sister at ease. This was not easy for Elisabeth either, as her husband, Michael, was also not there.

Both Katrina's and Elisabeth's husbands were part of the same battalion named the Mountain Hunters. On the day of Maria's birth, the Mountain Hunters had just arrived on the eastern side of Romania, alongside other Romanian soldiers, for the Third Battle of Oituz. This battle was a confrontation between Romanian and, to a lesser extent, Russian forces on one side and German and Austro-Hungarian forces on the other. It took place during the Romanian Campaign of World War I.

Four days prior to the arrival of the Mountain Hunters, the Austro-Hungarian 1st Army had already launched an attack against the Romanian 6th and 7th Infantry Divisions along the Oituz Valley. The main strike element of the Austro-Hungarian 8th Corps, which consisted of the Austro-Hungarian 70th and 71st Infantry Divisions, the German 117th Infantry Division, and the Austro-Hungarian 7th and 8th Cavalry Divisions in reserve, was ready to exploit any breakthrough made by the infantry.

The German 117th Infantry Division was tasked with advancing north of the Oituz Valley, while the Austro-Hungarian 71st Infantry Division was to advance south of the valley. The 70th Division was going to attack over the Ciresoaia and Pravila Peaks. The front was 7 kilometers (13 miles) wide, and at that moment, the Romanians were outnumbered four to one.

The extremely violent artillery preparation lasted four and a half hours. In the sector of the Romanian 7th Infantry Division, the Pravila Peak was assaulted four times by the Austro-Hungarian 70th Infantry Division. However, the 27th Romanian Division, on the right wing of the Romanian Division, held its ground. On the left wing, the 16th Romanian Division, pressed hard by the German 117th Infantry Division, had to give away 1 to 2 kilometers (0.62 to 1.24 miles) in the area, suffering high casualties.

Meanwhile, to the south, the 10th Romanian Division also maintained its position. Thus, during the first day of the battle, the Austro-Hungarian 8th Corps made a breakthrough in the central part of the front. However, during the night, the Romanian 4th Corps counterattacked in the German-held areas, taking two hundred prisoners and regaining some lost ground.

The following afternoon, however, the Central Powers resumed the offensive. The German 117th Infantry Division forced the 16th Regiment to abandon the area, and the Austro-Hungarian 70th Infantry and 7th Cavalry Divisions took the Pravila Peak. This forced the Romanian 7th Infantry Division to retreat to a new line of defense.

Violent fighting continued on August 10, and with the pressure on the 7th Romanian Division increasing, the Romanian troops had to abandon the area. Therefore, for the Romanians, the situation started to be critical. Three days of very violent fights had the troops in the first line exhausted, and since the reserves of the 4th Corps weren't there, Lieutenant General of the 2nd Romanian Army ordered the 2nd Corps to urgently send all its available reserves and asked for more troops from the Romanian General Headquarters.

However, at the same time, the 1st Romanian Army was engaged in a more violent clash at Marasesti with the German 9th Army, so all that could be sent was the 1st Cavalry Division, which arrived the following morning, while the Mountain Hunters Battalion, the first such unit in the Romanian army, and the Frontier-guard Brigade were on their way to Oituz.

German General Gerock, seeking to achieve the much-desired breakthrough into the Trotus Valley, engaged his last reserves to the battle on August 11. The 70th Infantry and 7th Cavalry Division launched an attack on the Ciresoaia Peak. However, the 15th Romanian Division managed to hold their ground, and the German assaults were held back. Despite this, several Austrian units infiltrated south of the peak, and the Romanian regiment had to retreat to avoid being trapped.

To the south, the German 117th Division again assaulted the Cosna Mountain but failed. However, several advances were made south of the mountain, which were stopped in the Oituz village.

But, with their backsides unguarded, the Romanian troops on Cosna pulled back, and the Gerock Group had managed to conquer the last two heights separating it from the Trotus Valley.

At that moment, Romanian reinforcements arrived, and two battalions attacked the Ciresoaia area, managing to regain some of the lost ground and establishing contact with the Russian 9th Army. At 1900 hours, the 1st Cavalry Division was also thrown into battle. It attacked the German troops with one brigade on the southern slope of Cosna Mountain, and with help from the 2nd Brigade, both objectives were secured by nightfall. Subsequently, the 1st Cavalry Division, sent by the 2nd Corps, counterattacked in Oituz Village with two armored cars, defending the units of the 117th German Division.

The danger had passed, but the advance of the German 18th Reserve Corps on the 2nd Army's left flank forced Romanian General Averescu to move a part of the reserves to the 2nd Corps. Despite the need to reduce his forces, the general decided to retake Ciresoaia Peak on August 12. The attack was carried out by the 27th Romanian Division, a battalion from the 15th Regiment, two battalions from the Russian 2nd Division (part of the 9th Army), and the Mountain Hunters Battalion, which had just arrived after a 99-mile march and started the attack after only a twenty-minute rest. To surprise their enemy, they did not prepare their artillery.

The Mountain Hunters Battalion admirably began to break through the defenses of the Austro-Hungarian

70th Division. However, before they could fully infiltrate behind enemy lines, Elisabeth's husband, Michael, was caught by surprise when a flood of lethal artillery shells fell on the area where he was stationed. Despite a warning from Daniel to seek cover, Michael sustained the full force of a mortar shell, which killed and buried him instantaneously.

The horrifying image quickly burned itself into Daniel's memory and created an enormous amount of guilt and sorrow from witnessing the death of his brother-in-law. No soldier from his battalion could help Daniel from the depression he began to suffer from.

Yet, the letter Daniel received from his wife, Katrina, a few weeks later began to help him cope with the horrific images that played relentlessly in his head. It gave him peace of mind and the strength to endure the deadly battle, giving him hope that he would one day get back safely to his family safely.

Dear Daniel,

> *I am praying every night for you to safely return home to us. And yes, this time, I said "us" because I am happy to tell you that I gave birth to a beautiful baby girl, and I am blessed to say that we are both healthy and safe. I named her Maria like you wished if we had a girl, and she was born on August 12.*
>
> *Looking at her reminds me of the person I fell in love with at first sight, and it certainly*

makes me miss you more. I look forward to the moment that I can hold you in my arms again, look into your eyes, and tell you, "Welcome home, my love." Please come back to us safely.

Your love,
Katrina

Lastly, a year later, the war began winding down, allowing people to be embraced again by the sun and peace they did not have in the past three years. Some of the soldiers were able to start returning to their families, while regrettably, many others had to remain behind to continue the never-ending fight from underground.

Fortunately, Daniel was one of the soldiers who safely returned home. December 20, 1918, was the day when sunshine finally lit up Katrina's soul again, and Maria could meet her father for the first time.

Chapter Two

After Daniel returned home, they all remained in the same house that sheltered Maria and her mother during the war, even though the house was progressively falling apart. The foundation began showing its weakness through the cracks that only multiplied over time, and it looked like the house was asking to be rebuilt from the ground up.

Daniel tried his best to keep the house standing as long as it could, but when he found out that he and Katrina had another baby on the way, he decided to start building a house for his family on one of the two pieces of land that he inherited from his parents right outside of their village. He knew he would have to build the house on his own, which wouldn't be easy since he could only work on it at the end of the week. During the week, he had to commute to the city and work at the steel factory, though he never complained.

Therefore, one piece of wood at a time, and after years, spring arrived with warmer days. Maria, along with her parents and her four-year-old brother Patrick, finally moved into their lovely new home.

The house sat on top of a small hill and was surrounded by plum, walnut, and crabapple trees. Behind it ran a small creek with crystal-blue water so cold that, at first touch, your hands would get numb for a short period of time. Despite the chill, the creek was home to countless fish that seemed to be racing against one another each day up and down the creek.

The creek became one of Maria's favorite places to be. For her brother Patrick, it became an enjoyable place only after Maria persistently coaxed and pleaded with him to join her there every day since the day they moved.

"Patrick! Are you still sleeping? Hey! Do you want to come with me and play? Let's go down to the creek!" That's what Patrick had to hear from his sister every morning for the remainder of the summer, and as soon as his eyes would open, Maria would hand him one of the handmade fishing poles that their father made for them, and then, she would excitedly drag him out of his bed to go outside.

However, that summer, Maria turned seven years old, and that meant she had only one more month left to coax her brother to join her by the creek. Before she knew it, it was her turn to be woken, but this time by her mother, with the long-awaited words, "Let's wake up! Today is your first day of school."

Thrilled to go to school, Maria jumped out of bed with joyous giggles and got dressed quickly in the school uniform that her mom had put on the chair next to her bed the night before. Then, after she dashed to the bathroom to brush her teeth and her hair, she went to the kitchen table and sat down.

"I am ready. Can we go?" she said to her father, who was pouring a glass of milk for himself.

"After we all eat breakfast, Maria," responded her mom as she was setting the table for breakfast.

"But Patrick is not awake yet. Do we need to wait for him? Could we eat breakfast without him so I can go to school?" asked Maria.

"What? But I am hungry. I want to eat, too," said Patrick as he appeared at the kitchen door dressed in his pajamas.

"First, you need to go back to your room to get dressed. Then you can come back down, and we will eat together. All right?" said the father with a smile on his face.

"Yes, Father," responded Patrick as he turned around to go back to his room.

"But I don't want to be late on my first day of school," continued Maria, knowing that they would have to wait for her brother.

"Don't worry, sweetheart. The time is only 7:00 a.m., and school starts at 8:00 a.m. After we eat breakfast, we'll take you to school with the horse and the carriage, so we'll definitely get there ten minutes before school starts," said the father.

While Maria was waiting for her food, she daydreamed about what might happen when she got to school. Suddenly, she felt a flutter in her stomach and couldn't eat by the time her mother put the food on the table.

"Father, can we go now? I am not hungry anymore," Maria said.

"Not before you eat a little bit. You need to eat something before you go to school," he responded.

Maria ate a few bites before her entire family took her to school in their horse-drawn carriage. Later, around 7:15 a.m., she met her best friend, Georgia, and her neighbor, Maximus, in front of her house, and they walked to school together.

Most of the time, they walked on the edge of the road made up of gravel to ensure they kept out of the way of horse-drawn carriages. Occasionally, they went along a footpath by the church along the creek that went all the way to the school, but only on hot summer days when they could splash their feet in the water and have their feet dry from the heat before they would arrive at school. Not that they would get in trouble for wet feet, but simply because inside the school, it was always cold, and their feet wouldn't get dry, as they all three have learned that on their own.

The school was built with medium-sized bricks and had windows all around it, but the windows were way too high to be able to see outside. Underneath the building was a cold, full-size basement that was used as a location where the local army secretly used to keep their precious ammunition and cannons during the war. Moreover, the school was situated at the base of a small hill and surrounded by old, tall oak trees that sheltered every inch of the school from any sun rays that could have otherwise helped to provide some warmth.

Therefore, by the time winter began knocking on the school doors, the children already understood the need for extra layers of clothing while in school, despite the fact that every classroom had its own chimney by the teacher's desk that they regularly fed with wooden logs.

But as the winter season grew colder, the bitter outdoor temperatures combined with the chill coming from the basement made it seem as if every effort to feed the fire and keep the room warm was futile. As a result, a few children began to stand and move around to warm themselves up.

"What are you children doing? This is not gym class. Sit back down immediately!" yelled the teacher when she noticed some of the students standing up and moving around.

Their teacher, Ms. Clara, couldn't realize how cold the classroom had become because she was constantly walking back and forth between the rows of desks.

"But, Ms. Clara . . ." Maria tried to explain.

"There is no 'But, Ms. Clara'! I told you to sit down and pay attention!"

But once the entire classroom stood up and began marching in place to get warm, that's when Ms. Clara realized that the chimney wasn't producing enough heat to keep the children warm. So she decided to send the children home early and told them not to return to school until next week when the weather was supposed to be a bit warmer.

Lucky for them, winter vacation was soon approaching, so they didn't have to endure the bitter temperature at school for much longer. Lucky for Maria, winter vacation brought her favorite time of year: Christmas. The Christmas traditions for Maria's family were already set. It all started with a delicious Christmas Eve dinner while her father told the story of Christmas for all to hear. Then, the entire family would gather around the Christmas tree, where gifts were waiting to be opened.

Additionally, starting that year, there was a new addition to their family, a boy named Adam, Patrick and Maria's new baby brother. So that year, more gifts were to be found underneath the tree.

The only people who spent time with Maria's family during the holidays were Mia with her husband and, of course, Elisabeth, Katrina's sister.

Mia, a truly pleasant lady, was Katrina and Elisabeth's aunt who raised them both from a very young age since her sister died while giving birth to Katrina. Their father died after a short time as his health was slowly failing from a broken heart.

Also, the children never had a chance to meet their father's parents since they were killed during World War I.

Altogether, they weren't a big family, but Maria, Patrick, and Adam's foundation was certainly pure love, and they all learned how to love from the best—their parents. Their mother believed in the idea that kids could be broken for life if they didn't feel valued by at least one adult. So she made it a priority to believe in all of them and always ensured that they believed in themselves. The best lesson they learned from their father was the way he sacrificed for his family. He always tried his best to do everything for his family to ensure that they had a joyful life. For him, family was the most important thing in the world, and the love he had for his family was like no other.

For that reason, each year, their family felt blessed to have each other during the Christmas holiday. Everything felt perfect to them, especially for Patrick, who got to open gifts on Christmas Eve and then more on December 28 for his birthday.

That year, Patrick turned five years old, and he had already started talking with enthusiasm about the idea of going to school. This was despite the fact that he began to hear his sister Maria complain to their mother almost every morning that she didn't want to wake up so early to go to school.

But then, on the other hand, Maria had felt the same as her brother Patrick. At first, Maria was excited about school, but after a few months, her excitement faded, and she wanted to stay home. After all, having to wake up every morning at 6:30 a.m. to be at school for seven hours, plus another hour and a half just walking to and from school, would weaken anyone's enthusiasm. Perhaps if the school days were a bit shorter, maybe they wouldn't lose their excitement so early.

However, the holidays had passed, and that meant winter vacation was over as well, and it was time for the children to go back to school. And even though Maria lost interest in going to school, she was still eager to meet her friends Maximus and Georgia.

Chapter Three

The night before school started, it began to snow so hard that Maria's father had to wake up a couple of times during the night just to shovel the snow that was piling at the front door, starting to trap them inside their home.

"It's snowing!" Maria yelled after she looked outside her bedroom window, only to find snowflakes falling gently from the sky.

"And look at all the snow we have! I cannot believe it! I am going to have so much fun with Maximus and Georgia!" continued Maria.

"Maria, stop yelling. You're going to wake everyone up. Plus, your father is still asleep. Get dressed and come have breakfast with me before you leave for school," said her mother as she rushed toward Maria's bedroom so she could stop her from yelling.

"All right, Mother," responded Maria quietly as she began getting ready for school.

By the time she got to the kitchen table, her breakfast was already waiting for her, but she didn't even plop down on her chair like she usually did before she could hear someone outside yelling her name.

"Maria! Maria!"

Maria quickly went to the kitchen window and saw that her friends, Maximus and Georgia, were already outside waiting for her.

"Come on, Maria. Let's go. We're going to be late," continued Maximus, yelling at Maria as he saw her through the window, but that time much louder.

"I'm coming out right now," responded Maria as she began waving at him with a big smile on her face.

Maria turned around, gave her mom a kiss on her cheek, and went to the front door, where she put on her boots as quickly as she could.

"I will see you after school. I love you!" said Maria to her mother as she grabbed her backpack and opened the door to run outside to her friends.

But she didn't reach her friends before she could hear her mother yelling at her from the kitchen window.

"Hey, sweetheart! , didn't you forget something?"

"Not really, Mom! I love you. I'll see you later," responded Maria as she continued walking without even turning her head toward the kitchen window.

"Maria! Come back inside the house right away, you silly girl."

Maria went back to the house, and as soon as she opened the door, her mother was standing in the hallway with a big smile on her face.

"Why did you call me back?" asked Maria with a bit of confusion in her tone.

"You really don't have any clue why I called you back, hm?"

"No, I don't have any clue," answered Maria.

But as soon as she saw her mother reaching toward the hooks where all the family winter coats were hanging, Maria then realized that she totally forgot to put on her winter coat before she left the house since she was so excited to see her friends.

Maria walked back outside to meet Maximus and Georgia, and she was surprised to see them waiting for her with a sled.

"Wow! That's a really nice sled. Whose is it? Is it yours, Georgia?" asked Maria.

"No, it's mine," responded Maximus.

"My father built it for me during our winter vacation, but I helped a little bit," he continued.

The base of the sled was fashioned from thick wooden slate, and the sled runners were made from metal bands that had been around some wooden barrels behind their house. Maximus's father cut and carefully warped them upward at one end so that the sled would ride easily over rocks and other obstacles.

From that day on, Maximus brought it with him every day for the rest of the winter, and they would take turns pulling each other all the way to school. The best part of the sled ride was when Maria, Maximus, and Georgia reached the steep hill leading down to the school. Despite the limited space, all three of them squeezed onto the sled. They would laugh happily as they slid toward the entrance of the school.

The children didn't seem to mind the cold days, and they were having a great time together with the sled. But they definitely enjoyed the warmer days more because it was more enjoyable to walk to school. However, without a shred of doubt, the one memory that they would never forget would be the very last day of that school year.

As the last bell rang, every child quickly grabbed their backpacks and excitedly rushed outside of their classrooms while yelling happily out loud in the hallway, "Yes! School's out for summer!"

Maria, Maximus, and Georgia immediately joined the other children as well, chanting, "School's out for summer!" as they began skipping through the hallway on their way outside. They continued skipping on the way to their homes with huge smiles on their faces.

They didn't even mind the light rain that started to sprinkle small droplets of water on them. At the time, none of them cared too much because they enjoyed how it cooled them off a little bit, but soon, a few more dark clouds started forming in the sky.

"Hopefully, it doesn't rain any harder before we get home," said Georgia.

However, against Georgia's wishes, every drop of rain quickly began multiplying, causing the children to switch from skipping to running all the way to Maria's house.

"You should probably stay at my house until the rain stops," said Maria to Maximus and Georgia once they arrived in front of Maria's house.

But before they could answer, Maria's mother quickly opened the front door.

"Maria, I am glad that you are back from school. I have to go to your grandaunt Mia's house right now. She doesn't feel well," she said.

"And why are you children still standing outside in the rain? Why don't you all come inside the house? And while I am gone, please take care of your little brothers, especially Adam. You know that if you don't watch him for a second, he will disappear. Plus, your father should come home from work soon. Can you please do that for me, Maria?" continued Katrina as she grabbed her umbrella and left the house in a hurry without waiting for an answer from Maria.

Meanwhile, the rain started coming down faster and harder, and the drops were the size of a quarter.

"You can trust me, Mother!" shouted Maria as she watched her mother disappear into the thick rain.

Out of the blue, Maximus pointed his finger toward the house of Maria's neighbor. "Look at that!" he shouted.

"Look at what, Maximus?" asked Georgia with uncertainty, not knowing where to look.

But soon, Maria looked at what Maximus was pointing at. In a flash, her eyes looked mischievous, and she knew at that moment what she was about to do.

"What's going on, Maria? What are you thinking right now?" asked Maximus because he could feel like something was going to happen.

"Do you guys realize that's a cherry tree?" And that was all she had to say before they all started running in the rain toward the cherry tree.

"Hey! What about Adam?" exclaimed Patrick, reminding everyone of what his mother had said to Maria.

"Someone definitely has to stay with him," said Maria.

"No, we don't! Let's tie him up to a chair! We have done it before," said Patrick to his sister.

They all went back inside the house, and after everyone helped tie Adam to a chair, they rushed back outside to gather the cherries that were falling on the ground. However, since Mr. Peter's cherry tree was right in front of his house, they couldn't just walk toward it. They had to sneak along the side of his fence so they wouldn't be seen.

The cherry tree was so tall that half of its branches hung over the fence. Because of the heavy rain, underneath the tree, it looked like they were standing behind a waterfall, which created a flood of black cherries at their feet.

"This is the kind of rain I really enjoy!" exclaimed Maria with a big smile on her face as she held a handful of cherries. She watched everyone eat them quickly as if they were competing with the rain.

But suddenly, Maria's attention quickly turned toward her house.

"Listen! I think I hear someone calling us," Maria whispered loudly.

"It was probably Adam yelling at us from the house. We'll bring him some cherries, and hopefully, he will forget about everything we have done to him," responded Patrick with a smile on his face as he continued to stuff as many cherries as he could into his mouth.

"Then, let's gather some cherries for him, and we should all probably get back in the house," responded Maria.

But she didn't even have time to pick up a single cherry for her brother Adam before she heard her father, loud and clear this time, shouting for her and Patrick.

"Oh no! That's your father! He's already back home from work!" exclaimed Maximus.

"Maria! Patrick! Where are you?" shouted their father again with impatience.

At that point, the children started to panic.

"Good luck with everything, Maria, but I am not going back to your house. I am definitely going home," said Georgia.

"Me too," added Maximus.

However, Maria and Patrick couldn't escape going home. Consequently, the next day, both of them couldn't really tell if the purple color on their skin was from the rain of cherries from the day before or from the consequences of tying their brother Adam to a chair.

Chapter Four

Patrick started first grade after that summer, and he began to walk with Maria, Maximus, and Georgia to and from school every day. Despite the fact that Patrick was two years younger than them, they would always eat and hang out with him during their breaks at school. For that reason, Patrick quickly became part of their pack. Even though bullying wasn't a big issue back then in school, boys still acted like boys. However, they certainly knew not to mess with Patrick since he was usually seen hanging out with Maximus. Not that Maximus was a bad kid, but he was taller and bigger than the majority of the boys in school, and no boy wanted to be on Maximus's bad side.

As time passed, Maximus and Patrick became best friends and were rarely seen apart.

However, when the Great Depression began to hit America during the winter of 1929, as well as the rest of the world, Romania got hit just as hard. Many young people were forced to drop out of school to help their families in any way they could. In many cases, they had to drop out of school because of a lack of shoes or warm clothes for the winter weather since their families became too poor to buy them.

In Maximus's case, he had to drop out of school and leave the village to stay with his grandparents while waiting for his father to return from a job he agreed to take to support his family.

Maximus's father needed to work in a coal mine for six months. Unfortunately, two weeks after he began the job, there was a horrible explosion deep inside the mine. That prolonged his original contract from six months to an unlimited period of time. That day, twenty-five miners got trapped underground, and ten of them lost their lives. Sadly, Maximus's father was one of the men who died that day. Consequently, Maximus had to stay with his grandparents, who would now have to raise him since his mother died of pneumonia when he was only five years old.

The Great Depression was affecting families from every background. Maria's family felt it, too, especially after Maria's father was let go from his job during that winter. Without any hope of getting a new job, the money he saved vanished quickly.

Therefore, once winter ended, he decided to pull Maria and Patrick out of school so everyone could help work the other land inherited from his parents, located approximately five miles away from their house, on open grounds.

Sometimes, Maria's family had to learn to survive for days with only bread and milk from the one cow they had. But some days, their parents even had to skip a small portion of their food in order for the children to eat something.

Fortunately, by the end of summer, Maria's father was called back to work at the steel factory, which allowed Maria and Patrick to return to school. They were happy to bring along their little brother Adam, who would start first grade.

Maria and Patrick loved being back in school, especially to see their friends again. However, their everyday routine from home to school and back was making them miss Maximus more and more. Even though they had never stopped hoping that one day they would see Maximus again, time continued to fly by, and before Maria knew it, she graduated from high school. Still, nobody knew anything about Maximus.

Chapter Five

Since Maria graduated from high school and her nineteenth birthday was coming up, her grandaunt Mia thought of surprising her with a gift. She asked Maria if she would be interested in going with her to Bucharest, the capital of Romania.

"My childhood best friend Clara invited me to spend two months at her place in Bucharest, and I was thinking that you might want to come with me. It's going to be quite an experience for you, and we could celebrate your nineteenth birthday over there. I have already spoken to my friend Clara and your parents about it. So what do you think, Maria?" asked Ms. Mia as she opened her purse and reached for something inside.

"I would love that!" responded Maria enthusiastically.

"I knew you would say yes! Here, open this!" Ms. Mia requested as she handed Maria a medium-sized envelope.

Maria grabbed the envelope with both hands and held it high in front of her face for a few seconds, trying to take a peek through the envelope.

"Is it what I think it is?" exclaimed Maria happily as she began to tear the envelope cautiously.

"Happy birthday, Maria! I already purchased the train tickets, and we're leaving in two weeks," said Ms. Mia.

Two weeks passed by quickly. In the evening darkness, Maria and Ms. Mia waited at the train station in the city for the train that would come and take them to the capital. Once the sound of the approaching train could be heard, they began moving toward the platform. As the locomotive came clanging into the station, great clouds of steam billowed out from the belly, and a loud hissing sound was heard as the engineer applied the brakes.

Kids with their moms and dads huddled into little groups, getting last-minute lessons on how to behave on the train.

Maria picked up her suitcase, as well as Ms. Mia's, from the platform and carefully climbed aboard, beginning to look for their seats.

"Grandaunt Mia, I would like to say again, thank you very much for taking me with you," said Maria as she put her suitcase down on the floor next to her seat.

Soon, everyone was on board. The train pulled away from the station and quickly set off into the darkness.

There wasn't much to do on the train, so a few hours into the trip, Ms. Mia's eyes were heavy, and she wanted to rest, but the children that were across the aisle from her were restless and giggling.

"Hello. What are your names?" asked Maria, trying to make small talk with the children with the sole purpose of trying to keep them as quiet as possible for her grandaunt.

"Oh! We apologize if our children are being disruptive," whispered the mother of the children, realizing what Maria was trying to do. "It's just that it is their first time on a train, and they are thrilled to see their grandparents."

"They haven't seen them for two years," added the father.

"Do you know that it is my first time on a train, too?" said Maria, looking at the children. "And I happen to have a deck of cards with me. Would you like to play a few games with me?" Maria asked the children as she reached for the cards in her suitcase.

The children's eyes lit up when they heard they would be able to play some games, but after a couple of games, they slowly began to drift off to sleep, and Maria could finally go to her seat and get some rest as well.

Maria didn't wake up until morning, but as she opened her eyes and looked out of the window next to her seat, she could see mile upon mile of open fields leading to dense green forest and faraway mountains.

"So those are the Carpathian Mountains I learned about in school," stated Maria.

"Yes, they are. Would you like to switch places with me so you can have a better view?" asked her grandaunt, who was already awake and joyfully watching outside.

"Yes, please," answered Maria as she stood up, ready to switch places.

Maria and her grandaunt both enjoyed the beauty of nature, with its green forest of tall trees with long branches and wide meadows of tall grass filled with attractive flowers of every color. But the more time Maria spent by the open window gazing outside, the more the skin on her face was becoming red.

"Are you all right, Maria?" asked her grandaunt when she saw Maria scratching at her face.

"I think so, but for some reason, my face is itchy all of a sudden."

Maria's itch and reddishness became worse and more obvious, and the skin around her eyes began to swell, which caused concern for Ms. Mia.

"I wonder if you have an allergic reaction. Let me take a look at your face," said Ms. Mia as she pulled out a handkerchief from her purse and soaked it with some water from a small bottle that she had with her.

"Let's keep the handkerchief on your eyes for some time, and hopefully, the water will help with the swelling."

The water did not help much with the swelling or the itching, but at least it didn't get worse by the time they arrived at the train station in Bucharest. From there, Maria and Ms. Mia had to take bus number 25, which was the bus that Ms. Clara told Mia to take. It was the bus that would bring them closest to her home.

Since there was only one bus station across the street from the train station, it wasn't difficult to find. However, Ms. Mia was told that the buses were scheduled to run only every two hours. Once she realized they only had ten minutes to get across the street, they needed to hurry.

They walked as fast as they could outside of the train station, but before they crossed the street, they observed bus number 25 closing its doors and starting to drive away.

"Oh no, we're too late! Now, we'll have to wait two hours for the next one," Ms. Mia said hopelessly.

"No, we're not," said Maria as she brought her suitcase close to her chest, and after quickly looking in both directions, she ran toward the bus while she yelled as loud as she could, "Please, stop the bus!"

Fortunately, the bus driver had his window cracked open, and he could hear someone yelling at him. As he turned his head, he saw a young lady yelling frantically and running toward his bus.

Without delay, he put his right foot on the brake, and as he opened his window all the way, he began shouting at her as well. "Young lady, be careful! I heard you! I'll wait for you! Just be careful!"

Once Maria safely arrived at the bus, she thanked the driver for waiting for her.

"My grandaunt and I already had a long trip. We came all the way from Cluj-Napoca, and I don't know what we would have done if we had to wait two more hours for the next bus in this hot weather," continued Maria as she was pointing out toward her grandaunt, who was still cautiously crossing the street.

"Now, come on in, and please take a seat," said the driver once Ms. Mia reached the bus as well.

"I really appreciate that you waited for us," said Ms. Mia as she entered the bus.

"I am glad I could hear this young woman yelling to stop the bus. But now that I have learned that you are not from here, you can let me know where you ladies are going so you can relax without having to pay attention to each station, and I will let you know when we get there."

"You are a very kind gentleman. We need to get off at the station nearest the National Theater. Perhaps we will sit in these two seats directly behind you," answered Ms. Mia as she gave him a big smile.

Once they arrived near the National Theater, Ms. Mia knew exactly how to get to her friend's house. From the bus stop, it was only a fifteen-minute walk, and Ms. Mia remembered it very well because, on her last visit, she and her friend Ms. Clara used to walk a lot around that area. As for Maria, it was like walking into a different world.

Every house along the sidewalk was lined with trees in full bloom, and every house had a small garden of its own with many different colorful flowers. Each house was more beautiful than the next.

"Look at that beautiful house!" exclaimed Maria, staring at this beautiful house with French-style architecture, neat curved arches, soft lines, and stunning stonework that exuded rustic warmth.

"That is Clara's house. She does have a beautiful house," responded Ms. Mia.

"Her house must cost a fortune. Can I ring the bell?" asked Maria as they headed for the front door.

"Go ahead. But only once."

Maria did as she was told, and then they waited for Ms. Clara to answer.

Meanwhile, Maria couldn't help but notice the beautiful front door with its intricate stained-glass design.

Nobody answered, so Maria asked if she should ring the bell again.

"Let's try it one more time," answered Ms. Mia as she shifted her bag to the other hand.

Maria nodded and pressed the bell again.

"I hope Clara didn't forget that we were coming today," said Ms. Mia, smiling.

But the door opened, and a tiny ball of white fur snuck out of the house and wagged her tail excitedly, ready to play with her new guests.

"Phoebe! Not again! Come back inside!" yelled Ms. Clara at her puppy from the doorway.

The puppy quickly ran back inside the house when she was called but remained enthusiastic about her new house guests.

"Oh, Mia! It is so nice to see you again!" exclaimed Clara.

"Come here and let me give you a hug. The last time I saw you was probably twelve years ago. Am I right?"

"Can you believe it has been sixteen years? It was 1920 when I last visited Bucharest, right after the war ended," responded Ms. Mia as she hugged her friend.

"And let me guess. This beautiful young lady is your grandniece?"

"Yes, this is Maria, my grandniece I told you about. She has never traveled outside of Transylvania, so I brought her with me to offer her some big-city experiences. Unfortunately, her first memory of this trip is of the rash that appeared on her face while we were on the train. Could we take her to a pharmacy before we settle in, if possible?"

"We can walk to my husband's office, and I can ask him to take a look at it. But first, let's go inside and leave your luggage in the guest room," said Clara.

The house was even more impressive inside than it was on the outside. It started with a vast hallway that led them into a luxurious living room, where the center of the brick wall held a gorgeous fireplace with a large framed painting of a beautiful lake. From the ornate dining room ceiling hung a stunning chandelier made from hundreds of crystals above a large rustic dining room table made of chestnut planks and surrounded by big wooden chairs.

"You have an extremely beautiful home, Ms. Clara. Thank you for inviting me here with my grandaunt."

"Oh, you are very welcome, my dear. And, you know what? Since my husband's office is only a few blocks away, let's cool off with some freshly squeezed lemonade I just made before we leave. It is a very hot day, after all. What do you think?"

"That sounds very refreshing," responded Maria.

After they finished their lemonade, they all walked to Ms. Clara's husband's office, and Ms. Clara and Ms. Mia began to reminisce about the past. But once they arrived at the doctor's office, they needed to postpone their memories for later that day.

"Nicholas! It's me, Clara," she said softly, knocking on the office door and cracking it open to take a peek inside the room.

Ms. Clara's husband was talking on the phone but gestured with his hand to come inside as he wondered what had brought her there unexpectedly.

Ms. Clara opened the door all the way, and they all went in and sat down on the large cushioned chairs in front of his desk and patiently waited for him to finish his phone call.

"Hello, sweetheart. I apologize you had to wait for me," said the doctor to his wife as he hung up the phone.

"And, Mia, such a pleasure to see you again," said the doctor as he stood up and took Mia's hand to kiss it.

"It has been a long time since we saw each other. And let me guess? This beautiful young lady is your grandniece Maria? Clara told me that you might bring her along," continued the doctor.

"I am glad she came along," responded Ms. Mia as she gently put her hand on Maria's shoulder.

"Nicholas, we don't want to take much of your time, but the reason we stopped by is because Maria started to have a rash, or so we think, on her face as they were traveling on the train. And we were hoping you could help her," said Ms. Clara.

After a short examination, Dr. Nicholas believed that Maria had a simple case of heat rash. So he then applied a calming lotion, and her face seemed to look better right away.

"You know what? Now that Maria is taken care of, if you would like, you ladies can take my car and take this young girl for a tour of the city. I do have to stay here for a few more hours, and if you are not back on time to pick me up, no problem. I could use some exercise so I could just walk home."

Since Ms. Clara didn't have any plans for the day, she decided to take her husband's car and give Maria and Ms. Mia a tour of Bucharest.

First, they went to see one of the most beautiful pieces of art in the city, the imitation of Paris's Arc De Triomphe, which was erected in 1922 to commemorate the creation of Greater Romania that took place in 1918. The Arc De Triomphe had sites of World War I battles inscribed inside the arch. That year, the imitation, which was originally made out of wood, was replaced by stones.

Then, as they continued driving throughout the city, Maria studied the way the cars were taking over the streets and nearly hiding the horse-drawn carriages between them, allowing technology the right of way and perhaps slowly starting to leave the old ways behind.

On the sidewalk, Maria observed how men had stylish suits accessorized with eye-catching hats and shoes, and the women were dressed in attractive, colorful dresses with purses and hats to match. Their attires and hair, as well as the way they carried themselves, were very different from where she came from. Maria learned that the city's elegant architecture and the sophistication of its elite earned Bucharest the nickname of Little Paris.

Each day in the city brought new things for Maria to learn and discover. Since Dr. Nicholas and Clara frequently hosted friends for dinner, Maria also had ample opportunity to practice her manners.

Later that week, at one of the many dinners Clara was hosting at her home, Maria was given the opportunity to make some money from one of Ms. Clara's good friends, Ms. Rose.

"Maria, you know, our babysitter left us unexpectedly yesterday. If you would like to make some money during your stay in Bucharest, my husband and I would love for you to take care of our three-and-a-half-year-old daughter. We would only need you in the mornings," said Ms. Rose to Maria.

Maria thought this opportunity sounded very easy since she was already used to taking care of her brothers when they were young, so she happily accepted it.

"And if you decide to extend your stay in Bucharest, we will be happy to have you take care of our little girl as long as you want," continued Rose's husband, Victor, with a smile on his face.

Maria started the following day, and that made her time in Bucharest pass much faster. Before she knew it, it was time for her to return to her small village.

Nonetheless, she greatly enjoyed her new city experience, and since taking care of the little girl was practically effortless, Maria decided to extend her stay in Bucharest and accept Victor's offer to continue caring for his daughter. The offer sounded even better when Victor doubled her pay and offered her the option to live with them.

"Moving in with us would be more convenient for everyone, and you would absolutely save money by not having to find a place on your own to rent now that Ms. Mia has to return home," said Victor to Maria, which made her feel welcome in their home.

However, after only three weeks, Maria became quite uncomfortable with Victor's presence. The way he started looking at her was different from how he used to when she first met him, and that made Maria feel awkward and uneasy when he was around. But she couldn't say anything about it since she didn't know if what she felt was real or if her mind was simply playing tricks on her. She didn't have anyone to talk to because she was away from home for so long.

However, by the next Friday evening, Maria's unease around Victor proved to be justified, as she was putting the little girl to bed.

Usually, Victor and Rose spent their Friday evenings socializing with friends at a local pub and having a few drinks. They would come home once their little girl was asleep and usually entered the house quietly.

But the way the front door opened that evening, Maria realized immediately that something was not right. Whoever opened it slammed it so loudly against the wall that it caused a loud echo within the large stairwell, and it almost woke up the little girl.

Maria quickly walked outside the child's bedroom to peek from the top of the stairs at who had just slammed the door, and she saw that it was Victor. Victor was alone, and by the way he was stumbling in the entryway trying to take off his shoes, Maria knew that he had probably been drinking too much.

She certainly didn't want him to see her. However, as she turned to go to her bedroom, the wooden floor underneath her feet squeaked just enough to get his attention, and he looked up toward the top of the stairs.

"Oh good! Maria, you're still awake! Could you please come downstairs and make me a sandwich? I am starving!" Victor exclaimed loudly.

"I will, Mr. Victor, but could you please try to be a bit quieter? I just put your daughter to sleep, and you might wake her up," responded Maria as quietly as she could from the top of the stairs.

"All right! Then, let's talk in the kitchen," responded Victor.

Meanwhile, Victor grabbed a bottle of vodka from one of the top kitchen cabinets, and after he poured himself a glass, he sat down at the kitchen table and just stared at Maria as she prepared a sandwich for him.

"So, Maria, how do you like it here, in Bucharest?"

"I like it very much. It is a beautiful city. But talking about the city, where is Ms. Rose? Is she still out with your friends in the city by herself?" asked Maria, trying to release some of the tension that she could feel building in the kitchen.

"No. She is probably still talking outside with her friend who lives a few houses down the road," responded Victor right after he chugged the vodka from his glass.

Once Maria heard that Ms. Rose was outside of the house, she already felt a bit more comfortable knowing that she could enter the house at any second.

"All right, Mr. Victor. I finished your sandwich."

"Maria, I told you before—you don't have to call me Mr. Victor. Just call me Victor."

"All right, Mr. Victor . . . I mean Victor. Now that I finished your sandwich, could I please go back to my bedroom?"

"Of course. But before you go, could you please bring it to me?" asked Victor as he poured himself another glass of vodka.

Maria took a porcelain plate from the cabinet, grabbed the sandwich, put it on the plate, and took it to the table, where she placed it next to Victor's glass of vodka.

"Thank you, Maria. You are a very sweet girl," said Victor.

"You are welcome," responded Maria, breathing a sigh of relief that she could finally go back to her room.

But as she turned to leave, suddenly, Victor grabbed Maria's left hand and pulled her body close to his.

"What are you doing, Mr. Victor?" exclaimed Maria with fear as she quickly tried to push his hands off of her.

Yet, Victor only gripped her harder.

"You're hurting me! Please let me go!" continued Maria shakily.

Victor ignored Maria's plea to be let go. He aggressively pulled her onto his lap, starting to kiss her roughly on the mouth while his right hand moved up quickly under her sweater.

Maria realized that Victor's strength was more than she could wrestle against, and frustrated with not being able to free herself from his grip, she was about to scream for help when she heard the front door open.

Fortunately, Victor clearly heard it, too, so he quickly pushed Maria off his lap. Without any hesitation, Maria ran to her bedroom, locked the door, jumped on the bed, and began to cry.

"What's going on, Victor?" asked Ms. Rose as she watched Maria running up the stairs in such a rush without even saying anything to her.

"I don't have a clue," responded Victor coldly as he gulped down his vodka.

"Something had to happen to Maria. I have never seen her like that. Victor, did you say something to her?"

"Of course not. What could I have said to her?" asked Victor.

"I don't know. Something that could upset her."

"Like what? When I came inside, she was at the top of the stairs, so I asked her if she could make me a sandwich. And you know how Maria is—she is a respectful girl, so she did as I asked and went to the kitchen to make me a sandwich. But as soon as she finished the sandwich, she ran back into her room. Perhaps she might have been in the middle of something when I asked her to come downstairs."

Maria remained in her bedroom for the rest of the night, and because of the repulsive situation she found herself in, she decided that the next morning, she would quit taking care of their daughter. But when she was ready to tell Ms. Rose what had happened, Victor appeared to be waiting for her outside of her bedroom to beg for forgiveness.

"Maria, wait!" begged Victor as he watched her quickly close the door and lock it from inside after she saw him standing there.

"Please, open the door. I just want to ask for your forgiveness. Could you please open the door so we could talk before Rose gets back home with my daughter? Last night, I drank too much, and I didn't know what I was doing. Please forgive me, and please do not tell Rose what happened. I made a big mistake. I promise it will never happen again," said Victor, talking through the closed door.

Maria's innocence and lack of experience made Victor's apologies seem extremely sincere to her at the time, so she decided not to tell Ms. Rose what happened and to continue taking care of their girl.

However, the truth behind Victor's apology to Maria revealed its true face two weeks later. Maria was sitting at her desk in her room, writing a letter to her family to wish them a "Merry Christmas" and her brother Patrick a "Happy Birthday," when all of a sudden, she heard the doorknob twisting.

"Maria? Are you there?"

"Yes, I am," responded Maria with some concern in her voice, realizing that Mr. Victor was trying to open the door without knocking.

"What are you doing?" asked Victor with an irritated tone because the door was locked.

"I am writing a letter to my family. May I please have some privacy, Mr. Victor?"

After Maria asked for some privacy, she could hear Victor walking away from her door. She felt relieved and took a deep breath, then continued to write to her family.

But suddenly, *boom!* Mr. Victor kicked the door open.

The loud sound forced Maria to instantly jump from the chair. Her instincts to protect herself made her quickly push Victor out of the way so she could run straight out of the house.

However, Victor grabbed Maria's arms and threw her onto the bed with such force that her frail body bounced off the bed and crashed to the floor between the bed and the wall. Then, he pulled his belt off and grabbed her by her legs.

Maria's body was frozen in fear, but once she felt Victor's hands on her legs, she began to kick desperately. Luckily, she landed such a good kick on Victor's face that it left him on his back, breathless.

At that moment, Maria frantically stood up and jumped onto her bed, believing she had a better advantage to jump over Victor's body. As she landed just a couple of steps from the door, Maria only needed one more step to get out of Victor's reach. But just as she did, Victor quickly swung his arm and grabbed her right ankle.

"Where the hell do you think you're going?" growled Victor through clenched, bloody teeth as he pulled Maria down on the floor next to him.

"Help! Somebody help me!" screamed Maria as loudly as she could while she kicked wildly, hoping to break free again.

Only this time, Victor clutched both of her ankles and violently pulled her body next to his as he started to rip her clothes off and climb on top of her.

"No! Stop! Get off me! Help!" screamed Maria as she fought as hard as she could to free herself from him.

But Victor was too strong for her. He quickly put his left hand on her neck, squeezing her just enough to silence her while using his other hand to unzip his pants.

Maria kept trying to push him off, but the more she tried to fight back, the more pressure Victor put on her neck, leaving her nearly breathless. Moreover, the lack of oxygen made it almost impossible for Maria to continue fighting. Her head began to droop as she began to drift off to escape the reality of this horror.

Luckily, before Maria's innocence was taken, she noticed the pen she was using to write the letter to her family on the floor within her reach. She just needed to stretch her right arm out enough to grab it and use it as a weapon against Victor.

Therefore, with her last bit of energy, she reached for the pen, and without hesitation, she stabbed Victor's arm that held her throat. She did it with such force that the pen went through his biceps like a knife would go through butter.

Consequently, Victor instantaneously let go of Maria's neck, only to grab her neck with his other hand. As he tried to hold her down on the floor, Maria continued stabbing his other arm with the pen, again and again.

The excruciating pain in Victor's arm forced him to completely let go of Maria. Finally free, she was able to push him off and run as fast as she could out of the house.

Ms. Clara was the only person Maria could trust in Bucharest besides her grandaunt Mia, who had already returned home, so she ran to Ms. Clara's house without looking back. Once she arrived at Ms. Clara's house, Maria found the front door locked, so she started rattling the doorknob. Then she made a fist and began banging on the door while she yelled, "Help me! Help me!"

Dr. Nicholas was downstairs by the fireplace, reading the newspaper. He recognized Maria's voice right away, so he quickly rushed to open the door.

Maria was all wet, cold, and trembling, wearing only a thin dress with a sweater on top, both ripped and covered with blood. She had no shoes and just a pair of socks that were soaked from running on the snow-covered sidewalks.

"Oh! My Lord! What just happened to you, my dear?" asked Dr. Nicholas as he looked at Maria in disbelief.

But the second the door was wide open, Maria ran straight toward the guest bedroom without saying a single word to Dr. Nicholas. In the meantime, Ms. Clara appeared from her bedroom with a concerned look on her face, not knowing what was going on downstairs.

"What's happening, Nicholas? Who was yelling outside and knocking on our door?"

"Clara, you should come downstairs. It was Maria, and something had happened to her. When I opened the door, she just ran into our home as if she had seen a ghost. She didn't say a word to me, and she seemed extremely terrified."

"Where did she go?"

"She ran into the guest room," answered Nicholas as he pointed at the door.

Ms. Clara quickly made her way to the guest bedroom and knocked on the door.

"Maria? It's Clara. Are you all right? May I come in?"

Ms. Clara knocked on the door again, but since Maria didn't answer, she checked the doorknob and realized the door wasn't locked. She slowly opened the door, and when she saw Maria huddled in the corner of the room, crying and shaking uncontrollably, Ms. Clara took a blanket from the bed and wrapped it around Maria. Then, she lay on the floor next to Maria and began trying to calm and comfort her as she asked her what had happened.

It was nearly impossible for Clara to stop Maria from trembling, but her loving care helped soothe Maria eventually, so she could finally fall asleep for the rest of the night.

Once Maria woke up, she could hear an indiscernible conversation between Dr. Nicholas and another man coming from the living room. It instantly caused deep fear that triggered her body to tremble again. Her biggest fear was that it might be Mr. Victor talking to Dr. Nicholas.

Maria quietly got out of bed and walked to the door to lock it. However, once she realized that the male voice was not Mr. Victor's, she decided to slowly open the door to see who was talking to Dr. Nicholas in the living room. As soon as she saw a police officer sitting on the couch with Dr. Nicholas and Ms. Clara, she immediately closed and locked the door.

"Maria? Are you awake?" asked Clara when she heard the bedroom door close.

"Yes, I'm awake," responded Maria as she slowly opened the door.

"Could you please join us?" requested Ms. Clara.

Maria walked out of the bedroom, but she quickly turned in the opposite direction of the living room.

"Good morning, Maria. I am Officer Paul. Could you please come here for a moment?"

Maria turned around at his request, and as she started to walk toward the living room area, Officer Paul noticed that Maria was trembling even though she had a blanket wrapped around her.

"Maria, do you remember Officer Paul?" asked Ms. Clara.

Officer Paul was a good friend of Dr. Nicholas. He was also one of the guests at one of the dinner parties that Ms. Clara and Dr. Nicholas had at their house while Ms. Mia and Maria were living with them.

"Yes, I do remember Officer Paul," she responded as she sat on the couch next to Ms. Clara.

"Are you cold? Would you like me to bring you another blanket?" Ms. Clara asked Maria, feeling her body tremble.

"No, thank you, Ms. Clara. I am not cold."

"So, Maria, I'm here because Dr. Nicholas and Ms. Clara are very worried about you, and we would like to know what happened last night. Could you please tell us what happened to you last night?" inquired Officer Paul as he pulled out Maria's ripped, bloody dress from a bag that was on the floor, the one she was wearing when she arrived at Dr. Nicholas' house the night before.

At first, Maria hesitated to answer out of fear, but eventually, she began to explain everything, giving Officer Paul every detail of what happened to her at Mr. Victor's house. And then, after she asked Officer Paul if Victor would be arrested and put in jail, Maria was pleased to hear that Mr. Victor would undoubtedly not get away without being punished for his malicious actions.

Furthermore, after the events that took place at Victor's house, Maria never finished the letter she was writing to her family, and she decided to surprise them by returning home at Christmas time. She also decided not to tell anyone what happened to her in Bucharest because she knew that her family would be upset and angry. Since Ms. Clara did not tell Mia anything about what happened, as she had promised Maria, everything remained a secret.

Chapter Six

During the time Maria was gone from home, a new textile company had opened up in her village. So as soon as the holidays passed, Maria decided to apply for a job there. The only shift available was the second shift, Monday through Friday, from 2:00 p.m. to 10:00 p.m., and Maria did not mind working at night.

However, having to walk back home alone at night was something that she didn't feel safe doing yet. But since she still didn't say a word to her family about what had happened to her in Bucharest, she had to act as if she was the same girl that her family had known before: the strong and powerful girl who feared no one, even if she was broken on the inside.

Once Maria started the job, the work kept her busy. And with the chores she had to do around her parents' house, she felt like everything would work out just fine and her life could start heading in the right direction.

"Ever since you started the job at the factory, it seems as if you are even happier. You really do enjoy working there, huh?" asked Maria's mother as they were both cleaning inside their house.

"And by the way, tomorrow I promised Elisabeth that I would help clean her house and cook food for her. The doctor told her that she still cannot put any weight on her sprained ankle. It might take her one more week until she can walk. Will you come with me to your aunt's for a few hours first thing in the morning? If you won't be too tired," continued her mom.

"Oh, of course, I'll go with you to help out Aunt Elisabeth. You know I love her very much. But you know the main reason why I'll go with you is because I love you very much as well," replied Maria, smiling and winking while placing her hands on her mother's shoulders and staring into her eyes.

"You sweet girl. You know what? You should go and do whatever you would like before work today, and I will finish up cleaning the house," said the mother.

"Thank you, Mother. I think I'll go and start reading the book of poems that Georgia gave me for Christmas. But if you haven't heard from me by one o'clock, please come and check on me. Who knows? Maybe I will fall asleep reading."

"Don't worry, sweetheart. I'll wake you up if I find you asleep."

The book of poetry was a genuine pleasure to read, and Maria easily lost herself in it. She didn't realize it was already past one o'clock when her mother opened her bedroom door very slowly.

"I see that you are still reading. You know, I lost track of time cleaning the house, and I just realized that it is already twenty-five minutes past one," said Katrina to Maria, who was on her bed with her feet up on the wall.

"Oh, no! It can't be. Now, I might be late to work even if I go through the open field on Mr. Brown's farm," responded Maria as she hastily got off her bed.

"On the other hand, with all the snow in the field, I would be better off walking on the road, even if that makes me late. But, I might be asked again if I can stay overtime since they're busier during this time of the year, and perhaps everything will be fine," continued Maria.

And just as Maria expected, she was late to work, and she was also asked if she could work longer than her normal shift. By the time she finished, it was already midnight.

"Now I am exhausted. Plus, it was foolish of me to read my poetry book instead of taking a nap before work when I knew that I would have to wake up early tomorrow morning to go with my mom to see my aunt," said Maria to herself as she was walking toward the locker room to change into her clothes and go home.

To get home faster and get some extra sleep, Maria decided to take a shortcut that would lead her directly to the other side of the village. From there, she would walk through the open field on Mr. Brown's farm.

People didn't like taking that shortcut during the night because some areas were too dark, yet since Maria hadn't ever heard of anything bad happening there, she put on her winter boots, coat, hat, and gloves, grabbed her purse, and walked out of the building and went directly toward the shortcut.

Surprisingly, nothing seemed abnormal at that time. Plus, the fresh snow that fell on the ground throughout the day made the area a bit brighter.

As Maria continued walking, the evergreen trees along the pathway grew much taller, and their branches became denser. This blocked the snowflakes from reaching the ground and allowed darkness to take control of the area.

"Now I understand why people are uncertain about this shortcut during the night. And I don't think I will take it again at night," said Maria to herself as she began to walk faster.

All of a sudden, a sound similar to a sneeze was heard behind her.

"Who's there?" asked Maria with a quiver in her voice as she spun around, expecting to see someone. But she couldn't see anyone. The shadows only created more mind games for Maria.

"Hello? Is anybody there?" asked Maria again, but still no answer.

Maria felt as if someone was just watching her in the dark, so she began to walk even faster toward the soft light that she could see at the end of the path. The visibility was getting better, and when she saw two people appear in her way, Maria felt a little safer because she wasn't alone on the path.

But when they got closer, Maria realized the people were two men, and by the way they were walking, she guessed that they were probably drunk, too. So she stayed as close to the edge of the path as she could to try to avoid any contact with them.

Yet, as the men came face to face with Maria, one of them suddenly stepped in front of her.

"Hey, beautiful! Where are you going? Were you looking for us?" said the guy who stepped in front of Maria, mumbling his words while the other guy positioned himself beside her.

Maria could smell the alcohol on the man's breath, so she stepped to the side and tried to walk past him. But the man quickly stepped in front of her again, and this time he was angry that Maria was ignoring him.

"What? Are you deaf? Answer me!" the guy yelled at Maria.

Maria's hands started to shake, and her eyes were flooding with tears, and she feared what might happen next. She held her purse close to her chest with both hands and tried once more to walk past the man in front of her.

"Maybe she can't hear me because of the stupid hat that covers her ears!" continued the guy that was in front of her as he reached to pull off the hat from her head.

But reacting quickly, Maria leaned back just enough so the man couldn't reach her hat, which irritated him further.

"Oh, we have a feisty one, huh?" said the other guy.

"Let me see what you have there?" he continued as he reached for Maria's purse.

Frightened yet stubborn, Maria clutched her purse tighter against her chest, determined not to let it go. And just when she thought that the guy was losing his grip, a punch on the back of her head knocked her out cold.

When Maria opened her eyes, she found herself lying on the ground, and right next to her, she could see with blurry vision a fight between what seemed like three shadows. Suddenly, two of the shadows fell on the ground one by one. Then, the third shadow seemed to focus its entire attention on her.

"Please, leave me alone!" shouted Maria as she watched the dark figure come her way.

"I am not going to hurt you. I just want to help you stand up," replied the shadow, who appeared to be a young man and not one of the attackers.

Maria reached for his hand and allowed him to help her up to her feet.

"I believe this purse is yours," continued the young man as he handed Maria her purse.

Meanwhile, the men who attacked Maria were still on the ground, but one of them started to move his head.

"Do you live around here?" asked the young man.

"Yes, I live about fifteen minutes from here."

"Would you like me to walk you all the way home?" asked the young man as he realized that one of the men was getting up onto his knees and trying to stand up.

"Thank you very much, and thank God you were here. I don't even want to think about what could have happened to me if you weren't here," said Maria to him.

The young man offered his arm, and after Maria wrapped her arm around his, they both started walking without saying a word to each other. They only glanced at each other from time to time with a small grin.

But the silence was broken when Maria pointed her finger toward a house and said, "This is my parents' house."

"This is not possible!" replied the young man, with astonishment as he looked in disbelief at the house.

"Maria! Is it really you?" continued the young man as he took off his hat and turned his body toward her, looking straight into her eyes.

Maria never mentioned her name, and it surprised her that he knew her name. So she took a better look at him, and she saw a tall, handsome, dark-haired young man, but she still didn't have any clue who he could be.

"You really don't know who I am?" asked the young man with a huge smile on his face, which confused Maria even more.

"It's me, Maximus!"

When she heard his name, Maria finally connected the dots, and she realized the young man who saved her on the shortcut was none other than her childhood friend, Maximus. And she didn't take a second longer before she rushed to hug him while memories of their childhood came flooding back.

"I can't believe what time it is. I shouldn't keep you out in the cold any longer," said Maximus, as he realized it was already past 2:00 a.m.

"But I have a proposal for you. There is a play at the theater this Saturday, and there will be a ball afterward in the evening. I would love for you to join me. It's going to be entertaining, and we could catch up with our lives. Will you join me?"

"Yes, of course! I would love to join you," answered Maria with exuberance.

"Then, please, say hello to your family, and I'll be at your house early Saturday afternoon," said Maximus. After he gave Maria a kiss on her left cheek, he waited for her to walk into her house before he began his walk home.

That night, Maria struggled to fall asleep. Therefore, waking up in the morning wasn't easy at all. And even though Maria's head was definitely not in the present that morning after everything that happened the night before, she still kept her promise and went to her Aunt Elisabeth's house to help with some cleaning.

"You seem kind of troubled this morning, and you are very quiet. Is everything all right?" asked her mother.

"I'll be okay, but last night, I had another traumatic event. And thank God for Maximus," answered Maria.

"What do you mean by another traumatic event? And what do you mean by 'thank God for Maximus'?" continued Maria's mother as she put the broom against the wall and stepped closer to Maria with worry.

"It's nothing, Mother."

"It doesn't seem like nothing to me. What exactly happened to you, sweetheart?"

Maria started to give her mother all the details about what had happened the night before. However, as she got to the moment when Maximus came into the picture, Maria's eyes started to sparkle. She started feeling sensations through her body that she never felt before.

"Maria? If I hadn't asked you what happened, you probably wouldn't have told me what happened last night. Why?"

"I just didn't want anyone to worry. But I am all right now."

"Thank God, and thank God for Maximus. By the way, what happened to him? We never heard anything from him after the tragic death of his father."

"I really don't know. But guess what? He invited me to go with him tomorrow evening to the theater and a ball afterward," Maria responded with a huge smile on her face.

"That sounds great. I always liked that boy. He was always very polite," said her mom.

"But what about work? Now I am worried about you walking home by yourself. Tonight, I will have your father wait for you," continued her mom.

"I'll be all right. I am not going to take that shortcut ever again during the night. So everything should be fine. But if I don't feel safe tonight, I'll talk to Patrick and Adam tomorrow morning."

However, once Maria's shift was over that night, she wished she had asked her brothers to wait for her. It was almost twenty minutes past her shift, and she was still waiting behind the doors, looking through the small window, trying to gather some courage to leave and go home. The terrifying images from the night before were playing through her head, and waiting in fear was not helping her at all. Afterward, she knew all she had to do was push the door open and just start walking home. Therefore, she took a deep breath, pushed the door open, and started to walk at a fast pace.

"Hey! What's the rush?" asked a male voice approaching from behind her.

Maria realized that the question was intended for her, but she began to walk even faster without looking back.

"Hey, Maria! Slow down! Wait for me!" shouted the man.

When Maria heard her name, she looked over her shoulder, and she quickly realized it was Maximus.

"Maximus? What are you doing here?" she asked, hoping he was there for her.

"I couldn't let you go home by yourself after what happened to you last night," he replied. "I arrived around ten o'clock and wasn't sure if you had already left. I decided to wait, and I'm glad I did because I saw you walk out of the building. And look what I have with me!"

"Wow! Is that the same sled that we rode to school when we were kids?" asked Maria.

"Yes, it is! So what are you waiting for? Get on!" shouted Maximus.

Maria settled herself in the center of the sled, and Maximus began pulling it with speed. When they reached a small hill, he hopped onto the sled in front of Maria and began maneuvering it with his feet. Maria held on tightly, and both of them enjoyed every second.

Once they arrived at Maria's house, Maria's mother watched from the kitchen window for her daughter.

"Is that your mother?" asked Maximus.

"I believe so. I told her what happened to me last night, and she's probably been worried about me all day. She even wanted to send my father to wait for me after work so we could come home together."

Katrina couldn't tell who was approaching her house, but as soon as she realized that the person being pulled on the sled was Maria, she freaked out and ran outside, hoping that nothing bad had happened to her again.

"Maria? Are you all right?" asked Katrina as soon as she opened the door.

"Yes, Mother, everything is all right."

"I was worried when I saw you on the sled. I thought that you were hurt."

"Hello, Ms. Katrina. It's me, Maximus. Maria isn't hurt. But after what happened to her last night, I waited for her after work so I could bring her home safely."

"Maximus, I can't believe it's you. Look at you. I wouldn't have recognized you anymore," said Katrina.

"Come on! Let's go inside the house so you guys can warm up," continued Katrina.

"Oh, thank you, Ms. Katrina, but it's too late, and I better get going. However, I am coming back tomorrow evening to pick up Maria. But if it's all right with you, I would like to come a bit earlier to say hello to Patrick, Adam, and Mr. Daniel."

"Of course, Maximus. They will be happy to see you, too," responded Katrina. After thanking him again for his bravery the night before, she went inside the house to allow her daughter a private moment with him.

Maria and Maximus shared a hug, and the look in their eyes made it clear that they were both extremely excited to see each other the next day.

Maria even began going through her entire wardrobe as soon as she went inside the house, and then, she continued going through her wardrobe again after she woke up.

Meanwhile, Katrina watched her daughter try on all of her dresses. She realized that this evening seemed to be very important to Maria, so she went to her bedroom and returned with a box about the size of a suitcase. She handed it to Maria.

"Open it, sweetheart," she said.

"Just a moment, let me try on this dress again," responded Maria as she held one of the dresses that she had already tried on.

"Sweetheart, please open this box first."

Maria took the box from her mother, and as soon as she lifted the lid off, she saw a royal blue dress inside. She gently pulled the dress out of the box, and as it unfolded, Maria's eyes lit up.

"This is a gorgeous dress!" exclaimed Maria.

"It is yours," responded Katrina as she gently grabbed the dress from Maria's hands and held it against her daughter's body.

"I made it while you were in Bucharest. Try it on, and let me see if I need to tailor it a bit," continued Katrina.

The dress only needed to be shortened a bit, but before Katrina finished tailoring it, Maximus appeared outside their house, walking toward the front entrance.

"Maria! Maximus is here!" yelled Patrick to Maria.

As soon as Maria heard Patrick, she rushed into her mother's bedroom.

"Mother! Maximus is here!" she shouted at her mother.

"It is all right, Maria. I just finished your dress," responded her mother as she handed the dress to her daughter.

"And don't worry, you have plenty of time to get ready. The boys will have a lot of catching up to do with each other, which will give you enough time to get ready," continued her mom.

Just as Katrina said, the guys had a lot of catching up to do with each other, but when Maria stepped into the room, the conversation stopped instantly, and they just stared at her.

"You look beautiful, Maria," stated Maria's father.

"Thank you," she replied.

"You do look amazing," completed Maximus as he stared at Maria adoringly.

That evening, Maximus never left her side, and they danced and talked. Maria felt comfortable and secure in Maximus's arms for the rest of the night.

Chapter Seven

As the weeks passed, the relationship between Maximus and Maria grew closer and stronger. Maximus continued to wait for Maria every night to take her home safely after work. However, one day three months later, Maximus wasn't waiting for Maria outside after work. Since he had not mentioned anything to her, Maria decided to wait on the bench across the street from the main exit door where Maximus normally met her.

Yet, half an hour passed, and there was still no sign of Maximus. Therefore, Maria decided to walk home by herself, taking the usual route she took with Maximus, hoping to find him before having to go through the long, peculiar path through the park alone. The path didn't have tall bushes along its edges, but it was tall enough to evoke Maria's fear of the dark.

To Maria's surprise, once she arrived at the path, it wasn't as dark as she expected. Both sides of the path were lit with torches, which was unusual. But that didn't make Maria feel any safer, so she continued walking down the path apprehensively, unable to understand why it suddenly seemed so bright and safe. As the path turned to the right, Maria's life was about to change.

Right in front of her, Maximus was waiting in the middle of the path with a torch in one hand, and he reached out his other hand toward Maria, waiting for her to hold it. Maria was absolutely confused.

"What are you doing here?" she asked as she gave her hand to Maximus.

But before she could hear Maximus's answer, Maria heard footsteps approaching from behind, and she quickly turned around.

"Patrick? Adam? Why are you here? And why are you both smiling?" asked Maria, her voice filled with more confusion as her brothers stood there, not saying a word.

"Really? You're just going to stand there and smile?" she continued.

Then, as Maria turned around again to face Maximus, she saw him kneel down on his left knee, reaching out his right hand and asking her to take his hand. While maintaining eye contact with Maria, he said to her, "The reason why I am here, waiting for you in the dark and holding this torch, is because I would love to become your light for the rest of my life. Will you marry me?"

Tears of joy appeared in Maria's eyes as she realized that her relationship with Maximus had not only become stronger but was on the verge of becoming completely committed. She knew she was ready to give Maximus the answer he was waiting for.

"You've lit up my life since we reconnected, so I would love to have you as my eternal light. Yes, I will happily marry you!" responded Maria.

Six months later, on October 1, 1938, Maximus and Maria got married in the village where they both grew up, and their wedding began just like a fairy tale. The streets were not yet filled with cars, allowing horse-drawn carriages to arrive at Maria's home, just like in a fairy tale. Maria had a horse-drawn carriage arrive at her house with Maximus inside to bring her to the church.

Each white horse had a decorative wreath around its neck, filled with flowers of many different colors, and their tails were braided and fastened with a red bow. The carriage was followed by another carriage filled with musicians who played their instruments so loudly that they could be heard from miles away. Behind the musicians' carriage, Maria's family rode in their own carriage while other family members and friends were already waiting for them at the church.

During the ceremony, the priest joined Maximus's and Maria's hands with a special piece of cloth. Then, he placed a crown on each of their heads while explaining the significance of each action. As they drank from the common cup containing both water and wine, they were told to expect both good and bad in the future. After walking around the altar three times, they were told that this would be the beginning of their married life together.

But their fairy tale wedding wasn't over once the ceremony ended, as there was still so much more to come at the reception. There was lots of singing, dancing, and constant food service. Once the wedding was over, Maximus and Maria left together to go to their home, which was the house of Maximus's parents. They seemingly disappeared to spend all of their time together privately for the rest of the year.

As the priest had mentioned during their marriage ceremony, there would be good and bad times during their marriage. Maria couldn't wait to share her first piece of good news regarding their marriage with Maximus and her family. Christmas was just around the corner, so Maria decided to host Christmas dinner at their house that year, where she could share her news with the family as a gift.

In the meantime, Maria wasn't worried at all that Maximus would find out about her surprise before Christmas. Her gift was hidden in a special place and would only be revealed when the time was right.

Therefore, on Christmas evening, the entire family gathered at Maximus and Maria's house. As everyone sat down at the dinner table, Maria suddenly burst with excitement and shouted, "I'm pregnant! I'm pregnant!"

Everyone stopped talking, and Maximus reacted by quickly picking up Maria and proudly spinning around with her until he abruptly stopped and carefully set her back down on her feet.

"Oh my god! Did I hurt you? What was I thinking?" said Maximus fearfully.

"Maximus, I'm fine," responded Maria with a big smile on her face.

Maria's parents stood up and declared, "We are so happy for you both." Then they hugged each other.

Meanwhile, Patrick and Adam threw up their arms in excitement and yelled out, "Uncle! Uncle! Who's going to be an uncle?"

The whole family was elated about the news, and Maria felt deep happiness watching everyone happily discuss the future member of their family.

But again, as the priest said, both good and bad things should be expected in a marriage. Three months later, bad news was delivered to Maria's family when they learned that Maximus and Patrick had to join the Romanian army.

It was March of 1939 when Romania was forced to accommodate itself to German demands after a ten-year signed treaty of economic collaboration that granted the Germans extensive and exclusive rights to exploit the natural resources of Romania. Romanians were forced by Germans because Hitler knew exactly that the Romanian agricultural and petroleum resources would be crucial to his German war machine that was already expanding. That month, Hitler's troops were already marching into Czechoslovakia, where they took over Bohemia and established a protectorate over Slovakia.

Patrick was sent to Bucharest, the capital of Romania, while Maximus was sent to the west side of Romania to the Army Corps Border Division. The only form of communication between them and their family was through letters, which they never knew when they would receive or if they would even reach the correct destination.

With Maximus being away from home for months, Maria missed him greatly and was reminded every day of him by her pregnancy, but she was fortunate to have her family there for her. Maria's family regularly stopped by her house to help her with anything she needed, and Adam walked Maria home after work every day because he promised Maximus that he would.

However, the help Maria needed the most, which nobody could help her with, was the day when the light from inside her body shut off unpredictably.

Maria was at work, and while she was using her shears to cut a large piece of material, one of her female coworkers asked her with worry if she knew that she was bleeding.

Maria didn't pay attention when she grabbed the roll of material, and she cut her finger on the edge of the roll.

"It's not a big deal. I will get a bandage in a moment," replied Maria while wrapping her finger with a handkerchief.

"But I was wondering if you are aware that there is blood on the back of your gown," asked Maria's coworker with concern.

Confused, Maria pulled at her gown and saw the blood. Not a lot, but definitely enough to make her heart sink in her chest.

"Oh my god! I need to go to the dressing room."

But as she turned around, Maria could only take a few steps before she felt extremely weak and had to stop to regain her balance. Her coworker quickly grabbed Maria by the waist and practically carried her all the way into the changing room, where she sat her down on a bench.

"Maria, how do you feel?" she asked.

"I feel light-headed, and I think I am going to pass out," said Maria to her coworker.

Maria rested for a few minutes on the bench, but since the bleeding continued, she had to be rushed to the hospital, where she ended up with an emergency Cesarean section. However, her placenta had separated from the wall of her uterus, and sadly, there was nothing that the doctors could do to save Maria's unborn son.

Maria was devastated, and her life started to feel like it was shattering without Maximus around. She was worried that if she wrote Maximus a letter about what happened to her and the baby, the news would cause him harm, and she was terrified of losing him, too.

Gradually, with the help of her family, Maria became stronger emotionally and realized that Maximus deserved to know what had happened. So she finished the letter that she had begun writing while she was in the hospital and prayed that all would be well.

Maximus's response to Maria's letter didn't arrive until later that year, yet what mattered most to her were his words, which lifted her soul and reminded her of how much Maximus loved her.

My dear wife,

I am so sorry for what happened, and I am feeling extremely blue that I could not be next to you while you had to go through something that nobody should go through. Please promise me that you will not blame yourself for what happened. It wasn't anyone's fault. I love you very much, and I would do anything in this moment to hold you in my arms. I miss you, and I hope to see you very soon. Be well, my love.

Your loving husband,
Maximus

Meanwhile, the Romanian army needed to reinforce the borders even more because of a signed non-aggression pact between Nazi Germany and the Soviet Union that left the Romanians caught among German and Russian juggernauts.

The Molotov-Ribbentrop Pact was an agreement of convenience between the two bitter ideological enemies that permitted Nazi Germany and the Soviet Union to carve up spheres of influence in Eastern Europe while pledging not to attack each other for ten years. For Hitler's part, he only wanted a non-aggression pact with the Soviet Union so that his armies could easily invade Poland virtually unopposed by a major power, after which he could deal with the forces of France and Britain in the west without having to simultaneously fight the Soviet Union on a second front in the east.

The Molotov-Ribbentrop Pact was signed on August 23, 1939. Shortly after, on September 1, at 4:45 a.m., the German battleship *Schleswig-Holstein* fired on the Polish garrison at Westerplatte Fort in Danzig (modern-day Gdansk), marking the first military engagement of World War II. At the same time, sixty-two German divisions, supported by 1,300 aircraft, began their invasion of Poland.

The decision of Adolf Hitler to invade Poland was a gamble. The Wehrmacht (the German army) was not yet at full strength, and the German economy was still locked into peacetime production. As such, the invasion alarmed Hitler's generals and raised opposition to his command, leaking his war plans to Britain and France.

Hitler's generals urged caution and asked for more time to complete the defenses of the West Wall in order to stem any British and French counter-offensive in the west while the bulk of the Wehrmacht was engaged in the east. However, their leader dismissed their concerns and instead demanded their total loyalty.

Hitler was confident that the invasion of Poland would result in a short, victorious war for two important reasons. First, he was convinced that the deployment of the world's first armored corps would swiftly defeat the Polish armed forces in a blitzkrieg offensive. Second, he judged the British and French prime ministers, Neville Chamberlain and Edouard Daladier, to be weak, indecisive leaders who would opt for a peace settlement rather than war.

On the other hand, two days later, on September 3, 1939, in response to Hitler's invasion of Poland, Britain and France, both allies of the overrun nation, requested Hitler to abort his invasion of Poland. But Hitler refused to do so. As a result, Britain and France declared war on Germany, marking the beginning of World War II.

The first casualty of that declaration was not German but the British ocean liner *Athenia,* which was sunk by a German U-30 submarine that had assumed the liner was armed and belligerent.

There were more than 1,100 passengers on board, 112 of whom lost their lives. Among them, 28 were Americans, but President Roosevelt was unfazed by the tragedy, declaring that no one should "thoughtlessly or falsely talk of America sending its armies to European fields" and that the United States would remain neutral.

As for Britain's response, it initially involved no more than the dropping of anti-Nazi propaganda leaflets, totaling 13 tons, over Germany. However, they began bombing German ships on September 4, resulting in significant losses. The British worked under orders not to harm German civilians, while the German military had no such restrictions.

Two weeks later, the French began an offensive against Germany's western border. However, their effort was weakened by a narrow 90-mile window, enclosed by the borders of Luxembourg and Belgium, both neutral countries.

The war frightened everyone about what would come next and certainly instilled in Maria's brain the high possibility of losing the people she loved forever. Because Maria hated everything about the war, she and her family decided not to celebrate Christmas or the New Year until Maximus and Patrick returned home safely.

Chapter Eight

The following year, the war started to spread quickly, and it began to affect Romania as well. On June 26, 1940, the Soviets gave a twenty-four-hour ultimatum to turn over the regions of Bessarabia and Bukovina, which were regions under Romanian administration since Russian Civil War times (1917–1922). The Soviet Union had planned to accomplish the annexation with a full-scale invasion, but the Romanian government responded to the Soviet ultimatum by agreeing to withdraw from the territories in order to avoid any military conflict.

On the other hand, on July 5, 1940, Romania allied itself with Nazi Germany only to be invaded by its "ally" as part of Hitler's strategy to create one huge eastern front against the Soviet Union.

As a result, at the end of August, the Army Corps Border Division that Maximus was a part of was told to start heading toward the Romanian eastern border now that Russia occupied Bessarabia and Bukovina.

In order to get there, the Army Corps Border Division needed to go through the towns that were very close to Maria. Since Maximus didn't know what awaited him on the eastern border, he felt the urge to see Maria once again.

Maria had no idea that Maximus and the Army Corps would pass so close to her village, but if she had known, she would have been thinking about how to see him once more.

Unaware of their proximity, she remained focused on her daily routine, occupied with the basic yet necessary tasks to get through another day. However, things were about to unexpectedly change for her.

After returning home from work and finishing dinner, Maria decided to lie down on her bed and reread the letters she had received from Maximus and her brother Patrick. These letters soothed her soul and helped her fall asleep peacefully every night. Suddenly, a soft clatter outside the house caught her attention.

The clock showed 12:30 a.m., and she wasn't expecting anyone to be around her house at that time. Then, another clatter was heard. But this time, the sound was closer to the front entrance of the house, which put Maria on alert.

"It has to be an animal looking for some food," she told herself while trying not to panic. She stood up from the bed and placed the letters on her desk.

Maria turned the lights off in her bedroom, and the second she lay back down on her bed, she heard the squeaky hinges of the front door. It sounded as if the front door was slowly opening, so she quickly went underneath the bed, trying to hide.

Gradually, the wooden floor began to creak underneath someone's heavy footsteps that Maria could hear coming closer to her bedroom. Frightened, she could only close her eyes and pray for whatever it was to go away. Surprisingly, the sound of the footsteps totally vanished as they appeared to be ready to enter the bedroom, giving Maria the belief that her prayers worked and whatever it was had disappeared. But, as she opened her eyes, her body froze in fear. She saw a pair of boots in the doorway, looking like they were just waiting for permission to come in.

Mysteriously, as the boots started to move toward the bed, Maximus's voice came from nowhere into Maria's ears, calling her name, "Maria! Maria!"

Maria's body was shivering with fear that she would be found underneath her bed, and the soft whimpers that escaped her lips didn't help much either. So she quickly covered her mouth with both hands, trying to keep the urge to scream in terror inside and resist the temptation to yell for help.

But then, the intruder kneeled down to look underneath the bed, and as Maria saw a hand pull away the blanket, she closed her eyes and began praying again that nothing bad would happen to her.

Maximus's voice once again was heard in Maria's ears.

"Maria! It's me, Maximus. Don't be scared. Open your eyes," he said to her.

Maria opened her eyes, and she could not believe what she saw. Maximus's hands were reaching for her, trying to pull her out from underneath the bed. However, feeling like her mind was playing tricks on her, Maria tightly closed her eyes again while her body shrunk even smaller on the floor underneath the bed.

"Maria? Please open your eyes. It's me, Maximus."

At last, Maria opened her eyes, and her frozen body slowly began to soften as she realized her mind wasn't playing tricks on her. The two hands that were reaching for her were indeed Maximus's hands.

Very gently, Maximus pulled Maria out from underneath the bed and gently laid her down on the bed. After they hugged each other like they never had before, their bodies remained one for the rest of the night.

Maximus's Army Corps Border Division was positioned only forty miles west of Maximus and Maria's house. The army was supposed to stay in that area for only a few days before continuing to the east. Maximus had more than enough time to visit Maria and then return to his Army Corps to continue on the road together toward the eastern border.

However, as Maximus woke up the next morning, he and Maria noticed the village slowly flooding with Hungarian soldiers.

Apparently, two days before, the Second Vienna Award, also known as the Second Vienna Diktat, which was the second of two territorial disputes that year, arbitrated by Nazi Germany and Fascist Italy, allowed

Hungary to occupy and annex Northern Transylvania to their country without any other right of appeal.

So at that moment, Maximus was caught in Hungarian territory. He knew right away that his Army Corps couldn't continue toward the eastern border, going straight ahead through the Northern Transylvanian territory since it was occupied by Hungarian troops. They would need to go around its south and keep moving fast.

Maximus needed to leave the region and return to his Army Corps as soon as possible. His only chance to get to them quickly would be with a car, but everyone he knew didn't have a car. Maximus's only option was to try to steal one of the cars from the Hungarian army, even though it was an extremely dangerous option.

So as soon as the sun set and it became dark outside, Maximus took the horse and carriage of Maria's father and began circling the area from their village, hoping that the Hungarian soldiers and their officers would be gathering at the village's only pub.

The officers were the only ones with access to cars, but so far, the only men in the pub were soldiers without a trace of any officers. But as Maria and Maximus were patiently still circling the area, two headlights could be seen heading toward them.

"That has to be the car that we're waiting for," said Maximus as he quickly turned the horse with the carriage, positioning them across from the bar, hoping that the car would stop at the pub.

As the headlights came closer, it appeared to be two cars. Luckily, both cars stopped right in front of the pub.

From the first car, a Hungarian soldier stepped out from the driver's side and opened the back door through which a single officer stepped outside. Then, both men headed toward the front door of the pub.

Meanwhile, in the other car, the driver, who was also a Hungarian soldier, opened each of the back doors. Two officers stepped out of the car and headed toward the front doors of the pub as well, while the driver remained outside of the pub to smoke a cigarette, leaning against the hood of the car.

"This is it. It's time for me to go!" said Maximus to Maria.

"It is so hard to let you go, even if I know that you need to go. Please be careful," she responded with tears in her eyes. She knew the danger Maximus would be in and feared she might not see him again for quite some time.

Maximus gave Maria one last kiss before he got out of the carriage and slowly started to cross the street.

Maximus's intention was to go behind the car without being seen, sneak behind the soldier, attempt to get him into a chokehold, put him to sleep, and then steal his car. His plan seemed to be working well. The Hungarian soldier looked as if he was an easy obstacle for Maximus, but as Maximus was laying him down on the sidewalk, unexpectedly, the front door of the bar opened. The soldier who drove the first car was coming back out, so Maximus had to quickly grab the car keys from the ground and run to the other side of the car.

"Stop! Stop right there!" shouted the soldier at Maximus in Hungarian as he saw his fellow soldier on the ground.

Maximus got inside the car and drove away while the Hungarian soldier desperately tried shooting at the car.

The first bullet shattered the back passenger window of the car, while the next three bullets missed the car completely. The sound of gunshots immediately alerted the Hungarian soldiers and officers, and they all ran outside.

Maria had been watching what was happening from across the street and began to cry, fearing that Maximus might have been shot.

"What just happened?" asked one of the Hungarian officers who arrived at the pub with the second car.

"Sir, someone just stole your car," responded the Hungarian driver who fired at Maximus.

"So what are we waiting for? Let's follow him!" shouted the officer as he jumped into the passenger seat.

Meanwhile, when Maria saw the Hungarians leave to chase Maximus, she set off with the horse and carriage in the same direction they were heading.

Maximus was already way ahead of them, but the Hungarian soldier's driving skills were much better than Maximus's since he constantly drove for Hungarian officers, and in only two miles, he was right behind the car Maximus stole.

The Hungarian officer pulled down his window and began shooting at the tires, hoping to stop the car. The sound of gunshots made Maximus drive even faster in the pitch-black darkness. Unfortunately, even though he was very familiar with that region, as he veered around a sharp turn, he lost control of the car, and it slid off the road and flipped over, landing upside down.

The Hungarian soldiers stopped their car with the headlights shining on the wreckage and had their guns drawn as they slowly and cautiously approached the car.

"I see the man, and he is not moving. His head is bleeding. Maybe he is dead. I'll check his pulse," volunteered the soldier as he grabbed Maximus's neck with his left arm while his other hand was still pointing his gun toward him.

"He's unconscious but still alive, sir. Do you want me to shoot him?"

"No. Let's pull him out from the car, and we'll throw him in prison to teach him a lesson, as well as anyone else who tries to mess with us," responded the Hungarian officer.

The soldier pulled Maximus out of the car and, with help from the officer, tied Maximus's hands behind his back. They threw him in the back seat of their car even though Maximus was still unconscious.

In the meantime, Maria caught up to the cars and realized that they were parked close together with their headlights on. Not knowing if Maximus was in trouble, Maria started to panic, and she gave a command to her horse to begin sprinting to get there faster.

Suddenly, one of the cars started coming her way, so Maria instantly stopped the carriage to light the oil lamp that was mounted on the left side of the carriage so that she would not look suspicious. Then, she commanded the horse with a pull on the reins to trot away slowly.

Maria was hoping that Maximus would be inside the car that was coming her way, but her heart knew it couldn't be him because he would be driving away from the village.

Once the car was in front of her, the headlights were too bright for Maria to see who was driving the car. Since the Hungarian soldier had to slow down because the road was not wide enough for them to pass each other easily, Maria could be easily seen by the Hungarians.

"That's very unusual to see a young woman by herself here all alone. Let's ask her what she's doing here. She might even know who this man is that we caught," said the Hungarian officer.

The soldier stopped their car on the side of the road, got out of the car, and began waving his arms and shouting for Maria to stop.

"Where are you going?" shouted the soldier at Maria.

But Maria could not answer because she could not understand a word the Hungarian soldier was saying.

"I will ask you again! Where are you going, and what are you doing here at this time?" asked the Hungarian soldier, irritated that he was not getting an answer.

Meanwhile, Maximus started to regain consciousness and slowly picked up his head. The light from Maria's carriage allowed her to see a man in the back seat of their car, but she couldn't tell if it was Maximus.

"I don't speak Hungarian. I don't understand what you're saying," replied Maria nervously.

Without a doubt, they did not understand each other, so the Hungarian officer told the soldier to take Maria off of the carriage and check to see if she was hiding anything in the carriage. But when the soldier tried to remove Maria from the carriage by her left arm without her understanding why, Maria held onto the carriage tightly with her right arm and began yelling to let her go.

At that moment, the sound of Maria shouting brought Maximus back to consciousness completely, and as soon as he saw the soldier pulling on her arm, he yelled, "Let her go, you bastard!"

Maria couldn't be happier to hear Maximus's voice. However, there was nothing she could do to help him or herself.

Neither the officer nor the soldier understood what Maximus was shouting from the back seat. But the frustrated officer, losing all patience with the man, quickly turned around in his seat and started punching Maximus with his fist very violently.

Maximus's hands were tied behind his back, and he had no way of protecting himself. So he began kicking the car door, hoping to break it open. At that point, the uproar escalated with every second and affected Maria's horse as well.

The horse began moving uneasily from side to side, and it looked like it would not tolerate any more noise or chaos before taking off running.

Maximus, unaware of what was happening with Maria's horse, continued kicking the door. He landed a powerful kick to the window, shattering it. The sound triggered the horse's instinct to protect itself, and it took off instantly, pulling the carriage with such force that the Hungarian soldier had to let go of Maria's arm to avoid getting caught underneath the wheels.

"What the fuck are you doing? You almost killed me!" barked the soldier at Maximus as he opened the car door with broken glass and pulled his gun out from his holster, pointing it at Maximus's head.

Maximus stared directly at the gun, thinking that this was his last moment alive. Then unexpectedly, a sucker punch knocked Maximus out cold.

"Get in the car, soldier! Let's go. He already wrecked one of our cars. I will make sure he rots in prison," stated the Hungarian officer.

"What about the woman? Should we go after her?" asked the soldier.

"No. Let's get back to the base. She looked way too scared when she saw us. She probably lives in the nearby village and was on her way home. Let's go back to our base and lock this piece of shit in a room with two soldiers to guard him overnight, and tomorrow morning we will throw him in prison."

Chapter Nine

Maria lost her husband again. However, what was hardest for her was knowing that Maximus was thrown into a prison that was only half an hour away from their house, and there was no way she could see him.

It seemed like nothing good had happened to the people since the war began, and no one could be seen smiling and laughing as they grew more concerned about what would happen next. This only made Maria hate war even more. Moreover, by the beginning of November, even the weather started to wage war against the people, making them feel like prisoners inside their own homes that felt like jail, but still better than the small, filthy, cold prison cells where Maximus and the other prisoners were held.

However, as the weather persisted throughout December, twenty Romanian prisoners were chosen to shovel the streets clean while battling the extremely heavy, wet snow. Additionally, nine other Romanian prisoners, accompanied by three armed Hungarian soldiers, were chosen to move a bunch of chairs and tables from a storehouse to a place where they were setting up for a New Year's Eve party for the higher ranks of the Hungarian army.

Luckily, after three and a half months of being locked up in his grimy cell, Maximus was chosen to be one of the nine prisoners. Along with the other eight prisoners, he was brought by Hungarian soldiers early in the morning on the day before New Year's Eve to unbury the storehouse that was covered with snow. After that, they began moving the tables and chairs to the location where the party for the higher ranks of the Hungarian army would be held.

Nobody complained for a second about the cold weather or the work they were given because they were just happy to be out of prison and finally breathe fresh air.

"Everyone back in the truck! You're going back to prison!" yelled one of the Hungarian soldiers, pointing his gun at them once the Romanian prisoners finished moving everything needed for the New Year's Eve party.

"Come on! Move! It's time for you to go back to your sweet home!" yelled a different Hungarian soldier, laughing because he thought he was funny.

The Romanian prisoners climbed onto the back of the army truck while the three armed Hungarian soldiers continued to watch them, their guns aimed at their heads.

Once they were all inside the truck, they sat down on the cold wooden benches. Then, the soldier sitting all the way back gave a hand signal to the driver, and the truck took off. It was a twenty-five-minute ride back to the prison, and slowly, darkness fell outside.

"What's going on, Maximus? Is everything all right?" asked the guy across from Maximus.

"No. I would do anything to get out of here and see my wife," responded Maximus, who seemed lost in thought.

"Stop talking to each other!" interrupted the Hungarian soldier sitting right across from Maximus. "And I don't want to hear any—"

But before the Hungarian soldier could finish his sentence, suddenly, a loud explosion was heard from outside.

"What was that?" yelled one of the Romanians as the back of the truck started sliding from left to right.

The Hungarian driver did his best to regain control, but the truck slid off the road and flipped over into a ditch. The Hungarian soldiers and the nine Romanian prisoners were thrown around on the back of the truck.

Nobody knew what had happened, but as soon as Maximus found a gun at his feet, next to a soldier who seemed badly injured, he picked it up and swiftly knocked out the second soldier by smashing the back of the gun into his face. The third soldier, who appeared uninjured and still had his gun, immediately put his finger on the trigger, prepared to shoot.

"Watch out!" yelled another prisoner as he jumped toward the Hungarian soldier, trying to disarm him.

Unavoidably, the prisoner who was already in the trajectory of the bullet from the soldier's gun got shot and was killed before the other prisoner had a chance to put his hands on the Hungarian soldier's gun. But as the fight began, the Hungarian soldier still had his finger on the trigger and killed another Romanian.

In the meantime, the Hungarian soldier who was knocked out by Maximus unexpectedly stood up and jumped toward Maximus to get his gun back, and he couldn't have gotten involved at a more perfect time. Ironically, the soldier's body became the best shield for Maximus as the soldier's buddy, who was still fighting with the Romanian guy for the gun, shot the Hungarian soldier in his back.

At that moment, there wasn't much time before anyone could get hit by the bullets released from the Hungarian soldier still shooting aimlessly. So without hesitation, Maximus pointed the gun toward the Hungarian soldier and took a clean shot to his head. The soldier dropped dead, and the last danger that remained was the Hungarian driver.

Maximus slowly got out of the back of the truck, and at a snail's pace, with his finger on the trigger, he started heading toward the front of the truck, ready to pull the trigger once again if necessary. Suddenly, he could hear someone whispering his name from the direction he was heading.

Maximus was confused hearing someone call his name, especially since the Hungarian driver didn't know it, so he waited and remained still with his gun ready.

"Who's there?" asked Maximus. "Come out, whoever you are!"

"Maximus, it's me, Adam. Don't shoot! I'm coming out," said Adam as he slowly started to show himself.

"And don't worry about the driver. He is dead. He crashed through the windshield," continued Adam, pointing toward the Hungarian driver, whose body was motionless in the ditch with his head in a pool of his own blood that was very obvious on the snow.

"What's going on?" asked Maximus.

But before Adam could explain, Maximus saw a car with its headlights on coming their way.

"Adam, get behind the truck!" yelled Maximus as he pointed his gun toward the oncoming car.

"Maximus, wait! That's our ride."

"What do you mean 'our ride'?" Maximus asked, confused.

"Don't you think I'm here for a reason?" replied Adam with a smile on his face.

The car continued coming toward them. However, as soon as it was approximately thirty feet away from the truck, it suddenly stopped.

"Are you sure that's our ride?" asked Maximus while the other Romanian prisoners who were still alive started running in different directions.

Adam pulled a large red handkerchief from his pocket, and once he started to wave it in the air, the car began moving again.

The car stopped in front of Adam, and he took the front passenger seat while Maximus jumped in the back, where, to his surprise, Maria grabbed him right away and pulled him in for a tight hug.

"Maximus, this is Marcel, and he is a very good friend of mine. Without him and without his uncle's car, we couldn't execute this plan for your escape," said Adam.

"Good to meet you, Maximus," said Marcel as he stretched his right hand over his shoulder to shake Maximus's hand.

"I'm glad to meet you, Marcel, and thank you," responded Maximus as he shook Marcel's hand.

"But how did you find out that I would be out of prison?" continued Maximus.

Maria found out that Maximus would be out of prison the day before New Year's Eve from the bartender who was working at the pub where Maximus had stolen the car from the Hungarian soldiers.

The bartender was a Romanian neighbor of hers who spoke perfect Hungarian, and since that pub was the only one in the area, he always listened to what the Hungarians were planning. As soon as Maria heard about Maximus, she shared the information with her brother Adam, and they came up with a plan for his escape.

Adam chose the open field between the two locations for the ambush to take place because it could give them the time they needed to get away, but they also knew they needed a car for their plan to work. That was when Maria and Adam decided to ask Marcel to help them with their plan to rescue Maximus because they needed him and his uncle's car. If their plan went as expected, everything Maria and Maximus would need for their journey together was already packed at Maria's house. They knew they would have limited time before the

Hungarian soldiers began searching for the escaped Romanian prisoners.

Unfortunately, the plan didn't work the way Maria expected. Once they arrived back at their house, Maximus didn't approve of Maria going on the run with him because it was too dangerous. He wouldn't forgive himself if something happened to her. And even though Maria insisted on being taken with him as she reminded him that she already lost him twice and she didn't want to lose him again, Maximus had to keep his heart cold at that moment.

As he gave her a hug, he said, "Maria, you'll be much safer here. But one day, we are going to be together again. I promise you."

Meanwhile, Adam and Marcel were waiting outside in the car for Maximus and Maria to take them as close as they could to the border. Yet, the second the door of the house opened, only Maximus started walking toward the car. Maria remained at the threshold and could only feel her heart jumping out of her chest, then slowly sinking into her stomach as she had to watch Maximus get into the car and leave her again.

"Come on, Maria! Let's go! We need to keep moving!" shouted Adam at his sister.

But once he saw Maria wiping her tears, he realized something was wrong.

"Maximus, is everything all right?"

"It would be too dangerous for both of us to be on the run from the Hungarian soldiers, and it is better for

Maria to stay home. She will be safer here," responded Maximus.

"Then, what's the new plan?" asked Adam.

Maximus looked at Maria and couldn't resist running back to give her another hug and kiss before getting back into the car.

"All right, here's my new plan. I need to cross the east border, but reaching that border by car is way too risky. So please take me outside of the village on the other side of the forest and drop me off on top of the hill, right next to the train tracks. The trains always run at a slow speed where you'll leave me, and I will take the first train heading toward the east border."

"Why east?" asked Adam.

"I have to try returning to my Army Corps Border Division."

"And why do you want to do that?" continued Adam.

"I need to get back to them because I don't know how long I could hide from the Hungarian soldiers on their territory now that Northern Transylvania has been given to them. Plus, when I cross into Romanian territory, I don't want to be accused of deserting the Army."

"Then, we'll take you there, but we are not just going to drop you off and leave you there. We'll wait with you until the train comes," Adam insisted.

Once they arrived on the other side of the forest, the time was 2:30 a.m., so Marcel parked the car right on the outskirts of the forest, just enough for them to stay hidden while still fairly close to the train tracks.

"Hey, the railways are still covered with snow. That's a good sign. It means there haven't been any trains yet," said Marcel, after which he turned off the headlights, and they all remained inside the car. But two hours had passed, and still no train had moved on the tracks yet. One by one, they fell asleep from fatigue.

Suddenly, a distant train whistle woke Adam up.

"I can't believe it's already daylight," said Adam as he looked at Maximus and Marcel, who were still asleep.

Then, another long whistle blew in the distance.

The train tracks were still covered with snow, so Adam knew a train was heading their way.

"Maximus! Marcel! Wake up! There's a train coming. I'll go check which direction it is coming from!" shouted Adam as he opened the door.

Adam walked to the train tracks, and as he squatted down to put his ear on the first track, he quickly stood back up and ran back to the car.

"Maximus! The train is coming from the west. That's your train."

"So this is it!" said Maximus.

"Marcel, it was a pleasure to meet you. Thank you for everything you did for me. I will remain indebted to you my entire life, and I hope you will not get in too much trouble for borrowing your uncle's car," continued Maximus as he shook Marcel's hand.

"It was a pleasure to meet you, too. And I am very glad that everything worked out well," responded Marcel.

Maximus grabbed his backpack and stepped outside of the car with Adam. As soon as they were out, Marcel reversed the car a little further into the forest so no one could see it from the railway.

"All right, Adam. Before you get back into the car, I need you to promise me something."

"Anything. What do you need?" said Adam.

"I want you to look after Maria for me," said Maximus as he reached out for one more hug from his brother-in-law.

"I will, and be safe, Maximus."

Adam walked back to the car while Maximus hid behind a tree until the train came. As Maximus expected, the train was going really slowly as it was coming up the hill. Therefore, it was not difficult for him to jump onto the train. Yet, once he was on the train, Maximus had to attempt to open several doors that were locked or jammed before he found a door that slid open easily.

But then, as he continued his journey toward the border, Maximus couldn't hide in the train because there were way too many Hungarian soldiers with canines waiting at the station. He had to leave the train way before he would get to the border, and he had to jump into an open field that met the base of the Carpathian Mountains. Then, after he safely crossed it, he still had to cross the mountain by facing the dangers that come with nature in the mountains to get back to his Army Corps Border Division.

Luckily, Maximus safely crossed the wide-open field. However, right before the last stretch, a group of six Hungarian soldiers appeared to be guarding the area at the base of the mountain. So, Maximus could use his gun to take them down with a high probability that if he did, that would bring more soldiers, or he could try tiptoeing around them at the perfect moment. But that would mean he would have to wait in the snow for an indefinite period of time.

It wasn't easy for Maximus to choose what his best option was in this situation, but it seemed like he didn't need to decide anymore because the Hungarian soldiers were getting ready to split up. Three soldiers went toward his left, while the other three soldiers went toward his right, leaving a clear path for Maximus to easily continue his journey safely.

However, Maximus still needed to wait for the soldiers to separate from each other far enough for him to safely get to the base of the mountain. Before he thought it was safe to cross, surprisingly, one of the soldiers that was heading to the right said something in Hungarian to a fellow soldier. Then he turned his horse around and headed right toward the spot where Maximus was hiding.

"He couldn't have seen me here. They all would have turned around," said Maximus to himself as he moved out of the soldiers' sight, quickly hiding behind the closest tree.

The white jacket Maximus had on provided the perfect camouflage to blend in with the snow. But at the same time, he wasn't safe just waiting there, so he quietly climbed up the tree.

Apparently, the soldier was trying to find a private place to relieve himself. As he pulled down his pants and squatted down, he saw fresh footprints in the snow, which put him on high alert. The soldier knew that nobody else should be there besides him, so he hastily pulled his pants back up and started to follow the footprints, leading him to the tree where Maximus was hiding. The soldier moved slowly and deliberately along the path of footprints with his gun drawn and ready to fire. But when he looked behind the tree, he was confused because no one was there, just a backpack.

Maximus didn't take his eyes off the Hungarian soldier the entire time. So the moment the soldier reached for the backpack, Maximus didn't hesitate to jump out of the tree on top of him. He grabbed the soldier's head with both hands, and with a quick and brutal twist, he broke the soldier's neck, killing him instantly.

Everything happened so fast that the Hungarian soldier couldn't protect himself or pull the trigger of his gun to alert the other soldiers, giving Maximus a safe, clear path all the way to the base of the mountain.

From there, Maximus began climbing the mountain without the danger of the Hungarian soldiers. But once he heard wolves howling nearby, he knew that he needed to go faster so the wolves would not pick up his scent.

Fortunately, the howls grew fainter behind him. But Maximus continued climbing with fear that the wolves might still catch up to him. Yet, by not resting for his safety, Maximus became tired and weak with every step he took. His legs were becoming very weary, and it wouldn't be long before they would give up on him. So before the sunset took the warmth it provided and the temperature started to drop drastically, he knew he needed to stop and make himself a safe shelter for the night.

Therefore, with the small bit of energy he had left, he dug himself a hole in the snow, deep enough to fit into. Then, he gathered some pine tree branches to lay on the bottom of the hole and a bunch more so he could cover himself. Completely exhausted, Maximus covered himself and closed his eyes, and before he knew it, he was fast asleep.

Maximus only wanted to rest for a few hours before continuing his ascent of the mountain. However, he remained in a deep slumber until the next morning when the sun's rays pierced through the branches and illuminated his face.

But once he started to ascend the mountain again, the snow that accumulated overnight made it much harder for him to climb than the day before. Maximus began to trip and fall in the deep snow more often. But once he arrived at the top of the mountain, he expected his journey to be much easier from this point.

However, before he began his descent, Maximus took a little time to eat some of the food that Maria packed for him. Even though it gave him some energy, it also relaxed him enough to not be as attentive to his surroundings as he was before. So as he continued to walk through the snow with a false sense of security, Maximus's right foot fell into a small crack in some rocks, causing him to lose his balance. As a result, he started to roll down the mountain toward an abrupt cliff where sharp rocks were waiting at the bottom for warm blood.

Desperately, as he was rolling toward the edge of the cliff, Maximus tried grabbing anything to help him stop. Suddenly, his body hit a bump, likely a bigger rock, which threw him into the air. He landed on his back, and his backpack became wedged perfectly between two rocks just before the edge of the cliff.

Luckily, his backpack stopped him from falling off the cliff, but the thump he took on the back of his head left his body still.

Maximus lay unconscious in the snow for a while. However, once he regained consciousness and opened his eyes, he was bewildered to find himself lying in a bed under a wooden ceiling just a few feet above him.

He was completely puzzled at the situation, but before he tried to remember what had happened to him, he became sleepy again and drifted off to sleep.

The next time he opened his eyes, he saw a woman sitting next to his bed, washing his face with a small towel. Nearby, a man and two little girls sat at a table, silently watching him.

"What is your name, young man?" asked the woman very softly.

"Maximus," he responded.

"Who are you, and where am I?" continued Maximus.

"We are still in the mountains. I was out hunting for food for my family when I found you in the snow. You were bleeding and unconscious, and I couldn't just leave you out there in the cold. So I brought you here, into our home," explained the man sitting at the table as he looked for any kind of reaction from Maximus.

Maximus noticed the man staring at him suspiciously.

"But what were you doing out there in the middle of nowhere by yourself with only a backpack that has a Romanian army uniform in it?" asked the man as he pulled out the uniform from Maximus's backpack with one hand while his other hand pulled out a gun from behind his back and pointed it toward Maximus's head.

Maximus was not only disoriented because of the head trauma, but once he had the gun pointed at his head, he became extremely bewildered.

"What's going on? You just told me that you couldn't leave me out there to die. And now, you are pointing a gun at my head for no reason. Who are you people?" asked Maximus as he tried to sit up.

"Do not move! Are you one of those soldiers who try to find us and then bring more of your soldiers here to kill us? Answer me!" shouted the man angrily as he put his gun right to Maximus's temple.

"What do you mean? I am not here to kill anybody. I am a Romanian soldier, and I am only trying to return to my Army Corps Border Division. I got caught and thrown in jail by the Hungarian army back in my village near Cluj-Napoca from the day we lost Northern Transylvania. But I was able to escape from their prison two days ago, and now I am just trying to get back to my corps," responded Maximus.

"You really don't have any clue what's happening over here, hm?" continued the man as he pulled his gun away from Maximus's temple.

"I spent four months in prison, and we were unaware of anything happening outside of prison. So I don't know what kind of answer you expect from me," responded Maximus, fuming.

But once the man started explaining to Maximus what had been going on, everything began to make sense to Maximus about this man's behavior.

They were a Jewish family, and Gypsy and Jewish families had to run and hide in the mountains because the Germans, with the help of some Romanian soldiers, were already building ghettos in those territories for all of them, only to separate them from the rest of the people. And because it was only a matter of time before the Gypsies and the Jewish families would all be deported or murdered, they were all forced to run and hide in the mountains. Throughout the area, they started to form small communities, where they all built small wooden houses to live in, and they all had to work together for their safety.

During the day, several men gathered to observe the area for possible intruders, while others went hunting to provide food for their families. Meanwhile, the women stayed home to cook and watch over their children, who played innocently outside, unaware of the danger around them. And if any soldiers were seen outside their area, that was considered a great danger for them; the soldiers would have to be killed for their safety.

So now that Maximus had learned what was happening in that region, he felt extremely lucky that the Jewish man spared his life, took him inside their home, and then allowed him to continue his journey toward his Army Corps Border Division.

The following day, Maximus began descending the mountain, wearing his regular clothes. The food that the Jewish family gave him before he left played an important role in his "escape" from the region. Once he safely arrived at the base of the Carpathian Mountains, he changed into his uniform and walked to the train station. From there, he took a train to the Russian border, where his Army Corps Border Division was already stationed, as he had anticipated.

None of his fellow soldiers could believe their eyes when they saw Maximus because they thought he was dead or had deserted the army since he did not return as he had promised his commander.

However, after explaining all the events he had experienced in order to get back, not only did Maximus escape punishment for his disappearance, but his fellow soldiers, including his commander, began to see him as a very brave man.

The Army Corps Border Division remained in those territories for a couple more months. However, starting in June, alongside other Romanian battalions, they had to join Germany's army to invade the Soviet Union. Their main objective was to occupy the city of Odessa, which had a large Jewish population of approximately 180,000, accounting for 30 percent of the city's total population.

The city was subjected to German aerial bombing from the very first day of the Axis invasion, and with three sides of the city surrounded, the Axis leadership initially believed that the city would fall quickly.

However, the Soviet Black Sea Fleet was able to transport reinforcements and supplies into the city, preventing the city from being fully enveloped and blunting the first offensive. This led to a second Axis offensive that began on August 16 and was initially successful. However, due to heavy casualties, the attacks on the city had to be put on pause again for a few days by August 24.

On September 15, as Soviet troops began to fall back to the southeast toward the city, Romanian troops attacked and captured the heights northwest of the Gross-Liebenthal district in Odessa. The Soviet leadership in Moscow had to make the difficult decision to sacrifice Odessa and redeploy its defenders to protect other areas of the Soviet Union.

The Soviet Black Sea Fleet, through the first two weeks of October, evacuated 121,000 troops and civilians, 1,000 trucks, and 20,000 tons of ammunition. Anything that could not be evacuated was sabotaged by the Soviets to prevent its use by the Axis forces.

The evacuation was completed on the evening of October 15, and on the following day, German and Romanian troops, including Maximus's battalion, entered the city of Odessa.

However, there were still between eighty thousand and ninety thousand Jews remaining in the city at that time. The rest of the approximately one hundred thousand Jews had either fled or were evacuated by the Soviets.

The German army and their Romanian allies started removing all the Jews from the adjacent buildings. After being rounded up, they were escorted by barking dogs and subjected to violent blows as they were taken to the city's central prison. There, eighteen people were crowded into cells meant for only one person, and they were not given any food or water. Most of them were women, children, and the elderly.

Consequently, on October 22, 1941, the building where the Romanian military commander's office and the headquarters of the Romanian 10th Infantry Division were located was occupied by the city. A radio-controlled mine, planted by the sappers of the Red Army before the city was surrendered by Soviet troops, exploded, causing the building to collapse. Under the rubble, sixty-seven people were killed, including sixteen Romanian officers, among them being the military commander of the city, Romanian General Ioan Glogojeanu, and four German naval officers. The blame was immediately placed on the Jews and Communists, and in response to the explosion, reprisals began the same evening.

Across the city, occupiers began breaking into Odessa citizens' apartments, shooting or hanging all residents they found without exception. They raided the streets and markets, shooting people who knew nothing about the bombing on sight, often against fences or the walls of houses. Then, on October 23, an order was issued threatening all Jews with immediate death and ordering them to report to the nearby village of Dalnik the following day. By the afternoon of October 24, about five thousand Jews had already gathered near the outpost of Dalnik, while another twenty thousand were led out of the city in a long line toward Dalnik. As soon as they reached Dalnik, they were tied together in groups of forty to fifty people and thrown into an anti-tank ditch, where they were shot.

Maximus's army corps had not yet participated in the cruel bloodbath, but Maximus realized the direction in which things were heading and decided to break two fingers on his right hand. This made it impossible for him to temporarily use his gun to kill innocent Jewish families, especially considering that he was saved from freezing to death by a Jewish family. Although the injury prevented him from directly participating in the massacre, it didn't spare him from witnessing the horror of the despicable and sadistic actions.

Furthermore, one of the German lieutenants became concerned that the killing would take too long, so the Jews were forced into four buildings. Holes were made in these buildings for machine guns, and after they were shot, the outside walls were sprayed with gasoline and set on fire.

The people still alive inside the buildings pushed and climbed on each other in an attempt to escape the fire through the high windows or through the hole in the roof created by the power of the fire. However, they were met outside by soldiers armed with hand grenades. It was an image that no soul deserved to witness, but the same thing happened the next day to the people in the other two buildings.

That night, Maximus not only shared his feelings with some of his fellow soldiers from his battalion but also conveyed them in the letter that Maria received from him a month later.

My Dear Maria,

I don't know how much longer I can hold on to my anger, seeing what's happening here in Odessa. I am very angry and sad that, after everything I've been through to get here, I am now forced to be a part of these cruel actions. The mass-murder operations taking place here are making me lose the strength to live day after day, and these innocent people definitely do not deserve this fate. I feel that I need to do something to help them, but I don't know how. I love you very much.

Your husband,
Maximus

Then, unexpectedly, two weeks later, Maria received another letter. However, this time, it was from the Romanian army. It stated that Maximus had been declared missing, and the only thing they found of his was his dog tags.

However, Maria's heart refused to believe that Maximus was gone forever. Something about his last words, "I feel that I need to do something to help them," in his final letter compelled her to find out more about what might have happened to Maximus.

Maria wanted to know who else from Maximus's battalion might have been declared missing and who might still be alive, hoping someone might know the truth or anything at all. However, since the war was not taking a break from oppression yet, Maria had to wait for the conflict to come to an end before she would begin searching for answers.

In the meantime, she continued with daily prayers and hoped that she would receive something else from Maximus or miraculously see him again before the war ended. But as time passed, she felt her prayers were vanishing in the sky before reaching their destination, perhaps obliterated by the war, like everything else.

And then, a year later, from the time Maximus disappeared in Odessa, Maria received a second letter from the Romanian army that said, "We regret to inform you that one year has passed since your husband Maximus was declared missing in the war, and we have to pronounce him legally dead. Therefore, along with this letter, we are including his dog tags, which now belong to you, and the official document of his death. We are extremely sorry for your loss, and may God rest Maximus's soul."

However, a death certificate and dog tags didn't convince Maria that Maximus was definitely deceased. She even refused to have a funeral service for her husband. Furthermore, from that moment, Maria decided to wear

Maximus's dog tags around her neck until she found out the truth of what happened to Maximus in Odessa, no matter how difficult it might be.

Chapter Ten

Two and a half years later, Maria, along with everyone else, was still waiting for the war to end. Yet, on the other side of Romania, in Bucharest, where Maria's brother Patrick was stationed, the war was just starting to devastate the terrain and the people.

It was April 4, 1944, when the alarms outside began to resonate throughout the capital for the people to take shelter. But since they didn't respond to the alarm seriously, believing the alarms were just another test yet again, many of them didn't reach the air-raid shelters before two hundred American bombers darkened the sky.

The air raid against the Romanian infrastructure served two purposes. First, the Americans wanted to aid the Russian ground offensive by destabilizing Romania and limiting the ability of the Axis to supply their frontline troops who were engaged with the Red Army. Their second objective was to prevent Romania from exporting its oil to Germany through attacks on both railway station switches and mining of the Danube River.

That day, the air raids lasted about an hour. Despite Romanian and German fighter planes managing to shoot down dozens of American planes, the aftermath was devastating. The streets of the capital were filled with bodies, internal organs, and intestines hanging from trees. Horses were shockingly thrown against walls of the buildings, charred corpses lay everywhere, and those with children who could not find space in shelters had to hide in basements of buildings, where many were crushed or asphyxiated.

However, the onslaught did not stop that day, and bombardment became an almost daily and nightly routine.

More attacks on the city happened on April 15, April 21, and April 24, continuing on the nights of May 2 and 3 when the British launched raids with seventy bombers over Bucharest. They returned with a hundred more heavy bombers on the nights of May 6 and 7. Then, one last attack occurred on the night of August 9, when the one hundred English bomber airplanes dropped their remaining bombs over Bucharest. They did this after bombing Ploiești, a city near Bucharest known for its oil refineries, on their way back to base.

That night, Patrick had just returned to his military base after a long and weary day where he and other soldiers from his battalion helped find people who were still buried alive under the rubble of buildings throughout the city. With his last ounce of energy, he could barely drag himself to his bed to get some much-needed rest before he had to wake up and start all over again looking for survivors the following day. Suddenly, the sound of the alarms began to warn the city that they were under a bombing attack again.

Patrick was already asleep when the ear-splitting alarms jolted him awake. However, he initially perceived them as background music in his dream. But when a loud explosion outside the base shook the ground, Patrick's eyes opened right away. He knew he had to leave the room to take shelter, but another thunderous explosion forced him to drop to the floor for cover. As he desperately tried to protect his head from falling bricks and shattered glass, a portion of the wooden window frame struck the back of his head before he had time to protect himself, instantly knocking him out and trapping him under a heavy rain of debris.

Some soldiers were trapped inside, while those who escaped waited frantically outside for the building to stop collapsing. They needed to start digging out the trapped soldiers before the next bomb attack.

Finally, Patrick was discovered amid small streams of blood, shattered glass, and a blanket of bricks. Still unconscious, he was dug out and rushed to the hospital. His injuries included a penetrating chest wound, a head injury, broken ribs, and a severely crushed leg. After doctors stabilized his condition, he was placed in a room with other wounded soldiers, where only time and faith could aid in his recovery.

Tony, a Romanian soldier and Patrick's best friend, was one of the soldiers who took Patrick to the hospital. Since he saw Patrick's health becoming worse, once he returned to the base, he decided to send a telegraph to Patrick's family, letting them know about their son's condition.

The news brought sadness and grief to Patrick's parents, and learning that their son was fighting for his life by himself in the hospital made them feel helpless. Moreover, not only were they witnessing their daughter Maria struggle to stay strong after Maximus's disappearance, but their son Adam had also been drafted into the army just a few months earlier and was sent to the eastern front of Romania—the same area where Maximus had disappeared.

On the other hand, as soon as Maria heard the news about her brother Patrick, she was not going to wait any longer for the war to end. She felt like the war was taking everything and everyone that was important to her.

"That's it. Tonight, I am taking the first train to Bucharest. I can't stand the idea of my brother fighting for his life without anyone by his side to take care of him," said Maria to her parents.

What Maria planned to do for her brother Patrick was very dangerous. Even though her parents didn't agree with her plans, Maria was already waiting for the train that would take her to Bucharest in the same area where Maximus took the train toward the east border. As her brother Adam had told her, it wasn't that hard to jump on the train. To her surprise, Maria wasn't the only one traveling from city to city like that. When she opened the door of a freight car, she found a woman inside with her two children—a boy and a girl—who were sitting against the wall. In the corner sat a man quietly by himself. Maria closed the door and moved to sit in the corner opposite the man.

The atmosphere was awkward, as nobody spoke. The only sounds in the freight car were of the children playing by the light of a nearby lamp. The adults seemed more interested in getting to their destination.

However, what was more odd than the deafening silence on the train was the lack of a toilet. If anyone needed to use the restroom, they had to quickly jump off the train when it stopped and then hurry to get back on.

By the next morning, the woman and the two children got off the train at one of the stations. Maria felt anxious about being alone in the freight car with the man, but she remained quiet in her own corner and patiently waited for the time to pass until her destination.

The man also remained quiet and uninterested in the other passengers. He didn't even lift his head when a German soldier jumped inside and began shouting at Maria, who couldn't understand a word he was saying.

"I can't understand you!" Maria repeatedly replied to the German soldier.

Since the soldier didn't understand Maria, he turned to the man in the corner and repeated his words. However, the man still didn't react or look at the soldier, which irritated him. It was clear from the soldier's expression that he expected a response. When the man continued to ignore him, the soldier decided to sit next to Maria and continued talking to her as if she would suddenly understand German.

"I already told you that I don't understand a word you're saying!" Maria said, but the German soldier kept talking to her anyway, making her anxious.

The man in the corner still minded his own business and didn't seem interested in what was going on. Perhaps he was deaf.

Meanwhile, Maria scooted over to show the German soldier that she didn't want him too close to her, but he didn't look like he cared.

"Where do you think you are going? Get over here!" shouted the soldier at Maria as he moved closer to her.

At that moment, Maria could smell liquor on his breath, so she asked him to leave her alone, using her left arm as a barrier between their bodies. But the soldier grabbed Maria's arm with his left hand while his other hand grabbed the back of her neck, bringing their bodies closer to each other.

"What is wrong with you? I asked you to leave me alone!" shouted Maria, and without hesitating, she pushed him so hard that the soldier lost his balance and fell onto his back.

"What the fuck did you just do!" shouted the soldier at Maria as he watched her stand up.

Angrily, the German soldier picked himself up and started to yell at Maria aggressively.

All of a sudden, the quiet man in the corner of the train stood up and spoke to Maria. "Just sit down in the corner, and no matter what you see, don't get involved." He then shockingly began shouting in German at the soldier.

Maria hadn't sat down yet because she was confused, but as soon as she saw the German soldier pull out his pistol and point it toward the man, frightened, she immediately sat down in the corner as the man told her to.

"Stand up right now!" shouted the German soldier to the man.

The man listened to the soldier and stood up slowly, but once he was on his feet, he quickly grabbed the soldier's arm that was holding the pistol.

Unexpectedly, the German's gun released its first bullet while the man was wrestling the soldier's arm that was holding the pistol and trying to keep it above their heads. The ceiling of the freight car took the first bullet, and seconds later, another bullet was released from the pistol, adding one more hole to the roof. But then, as the men continued fighting for the pistol, it looked like Maria was in the trajectory of the third bullet.

Luckily, a powerful punch to the German soldier's ribs caused the trajectory of the bullet to change its direction, missing Maria's body entirely. Then, as the men continued to fight, a powerful punch landed on the German's temple, causing him to drop his pistol and fall to the ground unconscious.

The man grabbed the pistol from the floor and, without hesitation, shot the soldier twice in the chest.

"Help me toss him off the train," the man told Maria as he opened the door of the freight car.

Maria couldn't believe what she had just seen, and she was tense and afraid and couldn't move. She was staring at the soldier's bloody chest while her mind replayed the scene over and over when he got shot.

"Come here and grab him by his ankles, and let's throw this piece of shit outside," insisted the man.

Maria stood up, grabbed the German soldier by his ankles while the man grabbed his wrists, and with a good swing, they tossed him out.

"Now, he will never touch another woman," said the man.

At that moment, Maria wasn't sure what this man had planned next, and her first thought was to push him out of the train while the doors were still wide open.

But then, she slowly began to step away from the door as she said to the man, "Look! I don't know who you are, but please don't hurt me. I promise that I will not say a word to anybody about what just happened here."

"Trust me. You are very lucky that I was here. After what I heard the German soldier say, it was very likely that you would end up where he did."

"Why? What did he say?" asked Maria.

"He said that he was going to rape you in front of me, then kill us and throw us from the train. And nobody would find our bodies. So I wasn't going to wait to see if that would happen. Besides, what are you doing on this train, and where are you going? You should know that it is unsafe to travel now while we are at war, especially by yourself," said the man.

"I am heading toward Bucharest, and the reason I am alone is a very long story," replied Maria.

"My destination is right after Bucharest, and since we're going to be on this train together for a while, I would like to hear your story," stated the man.

Convinced, Maria began to tell her story, and as she shared each detail of her life, it was as if she was dreaming with her eyes open.

The man was easily drawn into Maria's story, but after she unzipped her sweater to cool off a little bit, the man's eyes fell upon her necklace. Maria noticed the man's reaction and became uncomfortable, not knowing his thoughts, and zipped her sweater up again.

"Wait a moment! Where did you get those dog tags?" he asked as he reached for them.

Maria quickly pushed his hands away.

"Just let me see them," the man insisted as he tried to grab them again.

But Maria moved so the man could not reach her.

"These are all I have left to connect me to him!"

"Connect you to whom? What are you talking about?" asked the man, very confused.

"They belong to my husband."

Slowly, the man opened his jacket and pulled out his dog tags from underneath his shirt, and they looked similar to the ones Maria had. Then, he took them off, and with a soft smile on his face, he handed them to her.

"These dog tags belong to me, and that's my name inscribed on them. I was in the same battalion as Maximus, and we knew each other very well," said the man.

Maria grabbed the man's dog tags, and as soon as she saw "Army Corps Border Division" next to his name, "Alexander M.," she started to ask him questions, looking for answers about Maximus, even though the man seemed like he didn't want to talk about it.

The man spoke of places their battalion was sent and about fellow soldiers that he and Maximus got along with the best. However, as far as talking about Maximus's disappearance, it was obvious that he didn't want to open up, or perhaps he didn't know what happened to Maximus.

The man's lack of information about Maximus made Maria believe that he wasn't telling the truth and that he might be an impostor. Plus, the war wasn't over yet. Since the man was traveling on the train without wearing his uniform, Maria started to suspect that he might be a liar who somehow got a hold of those dog tags that coincidentally were from the same battalion as Maximus. And the more he talked, the harder it became for her to listen. So without worrying about any consequences, Maria began to let the truth out about what she was thinking.

"You know what? You should just stop with all the nonsense and leave me alone. Those dog tags are probably not even yours, and the only reason you killed the German soldier was to protect yourself. When I was yelling at him to leave me alone, you didn't even care. A true soldier or a good man would have said something right away!"

Maria could tell by the look in the man's eyes that he was slowly losing patience with her as she kept spewing everything she thought, but she couldn't stop.

"Perhaps you are a thief without any shame, and you're wearing the dog tags of a real soldier who might know who my husband is and might also know what happened to him."

But then, the man looked at Maria and said in a calm voice, "You know what? Maybe you're right. Maybe I am not a true soldier, but I am who I say I am, and I am the person inscribed on these dog tags. I am also the same person who unexpectedly took part in Maximus's plan on the evening of October 24, 1941.

"That evening, Maximus and I, along with six other soldiers, were guarding one of the four buildings filled with Jewish people to be killed later in the evening. Three of us were Romanian, and the other five were German. We were all posted on all four sides of the building. By that night, we could clearly see which soldiers on guard were indifferent to the massacre in front of their eyes and which soldiers felt terrible taking part in it.

"The soldier that was on guard with me was a Romanian soldier from a different battalion. On our left were two Germans, and on my right was Maximus with another German soldier. The screams of terror from inside the building were nonstop, and the screams became louder as it became darker outside. But as commanded, we were placed at the corners of each building filled with men, women, and children, all Jews, and we had orders to kill on the spot anyone trying to escape.

"That evening, on my side of the building, nothing was happening, but gunshots and hand grenades were heard from the other side of the building because some people were trying to escape. When we heard a single shot from Maximus's side, which seemed odd, we went to see what happened. Surprisingly, we found the German soldier lying on the ground with his throat slashed open while Maximus was heading toward the closed doors of the building.

"Maximus murdered the German soldier, but the soldier managed to shoot his gun one last time before he bled out. He was either trying to alert us or aimed at Maximus. It seemed obvious what Maximus was planning to do. Without hesitation, the Romanian soldier grabbed a hand grenade and prepared to use it against Maximus.

"However, I couldn't let that happen, especially after Maximus had opened up to me about his feelings the night before. I did what Maximus had done to the German soldier—I slashed open my own countryman's throat to save Maximus's life. And for that reason, maybe you are right to say that I am not a true soldier. But I had to follow my heart at that moment.

"Then I ran toward Maximus, and together we opened the doors of the building to give a chance to the people inside to escape. Immediately, people started running outside of the building, heading for the cornfield. Maximus took off his uniform coat. But before he could run away with the Jews, he handed me his dog tags and asked me if I could one day bring them to his wife in case something happened to him. So I took them and put them in the pocket of my coat as I watched him disappear among the people.

"But shortly after watching him run away, shots could be heard from around the building, forcing the people to drop to the ground instantly, followed by a storm of grenades. These added human hurdles for the people who were left behind. At one point, even a few soldiers were caught underneath the slaughtering rain of grenades while they were trying to catch some of the Jews running toward the cornfield.

"Anyway, that night was the last time I saw Maximus. I saw him disappear into the cornfield, wounded or not wounded, but his body was never found because we had to gather the remaining bodies later that night. The Jewish people who were caught, wounded or not, were thrown back into the building that same night. Moreover, that night, one of the German lieutenants, who was also a physician, decided to gather a group of soldiers and go hunting for anyone else who might have escaped.

"Nobody knows how many escaped that night, and I don't know if Maximus was killed by the lieutenant or his squad. But I do know that the next day, on October 25, three of the buildings, mainly filled with women and children, were all burned down to the ground, and the fourth building, which was filled with only men, was destroyed by bombs. There is no way anyone could survive.

"So because I knew that Maximus would be announced as missing the following day, I decided to return his dog tags to our Romanian lieutenant and explain to him that I found them on the ground while we were going through the dead bodies. I tried to make it look like Maximus might have gotten caught by a hand grenade while he was trying to catch some of the Jews who escaped. And now, seeing his dog tags around your neck, I am glad that my plan worked."

Once Maria found out the truth behind Maximus's disappearance, she wanted to believe that Maximus needed to hide in a place where he felt safe until the war ended. And then, perhaps, it would only be a matter of time until they connected again.

"But what about you, Alexander? Why are you no longer part of the battalion?" asked Maria.

Before he could answer, the train began to slow down as it approached the train station in Bucharest, and their conversation had to come to an end since Maria had to get ready to jump out of the freight car.

Maria gave him a warm hug and thanked Alexander for saving Maximus's life, as well as hers. Then, she jumped off the train and began walking toward the hospital, where she believed she would find her brother Patrick.

Chapter Eleven

At last, after a long walk where Maria had to be cautious walking on the extremely perilous sidewalks because there were many cracked buildings that remained standing even after being bombed, Maria safely arrived in front of the hospital.

"Please, God, let me find my brother alive!" she said to herself as she stopped for a second before she opened the doors to enter the hospital.

"Excuse me, young lady!" called a male voice from behind her.

"Oh!" said Maria as she quickly stepped aside.

"I didn't mean to scare you, but you seem kind of lost. Are you all right?" continued the man, who looked as if he was in his seventies. Because of his white outfit, Maria wondered if he worked at that hospital.

"Yes, I am all right. I was just getting ready to go inside and find my brother Patrick."

"Are you looking for a young man from Transylvania?" asked the old man.

"Yes. Do you know him? Is he all right?" asked Maria.

"I am one of the men who take food to wounded soldiers in the hospital. I think I know everyone who comes and goes from this hospital. Right now, Patrick is on the first floor of this building. Take the stairs, turn right, and you should find him in the room that is all the way at the end of the hallway."

Forgetting her manners, Maria stopped listening to the man once she learned where her brother was, and she began running toward his room. But as soon as she got to the end of the hallway, she realized there were two rooms across from each other, and both rooms were full of wounded soldiers.

She chose to go into the room on the right, but Patrick was not one of the wounded soldiers in that room. So she crossed the hall and walked into the other room where Maria didn't need much time before she saw her brother.

Thrilled to finally see her brother again, Maria rushed over to him and called out, "Patrick! Patrick!" but sadly, the sound of her voice only startled him.

Patrick was lying on his back in the bed by a window, staring at the ceiling as if he were dreaming with his eyes open. His face was ghostly white, and beads of perspiration dotted his face. The bandages wrapped around his left leg were saturated with pus and blood, while his foot was dark purple.

"Look at that dark sky with all those beautiful stars," Patrick whispered aloud.

"Patrick? It's me, Maria," she said as she grabbed his hand.

His hand was burning hot, and after feeling his forehead, it was obvious he had an extremely high fever.

Patrick couldn't realize that the woman next to him was his own sister. Yet as he grabbed Maria's hand and pulled it toward his chest, he said to her very softly, "Please, stay with me."

"Don't worry, brother. I'm here, and I'm not going anywhere," responded Maria, tears in her eyes.

Maria grabbed a piece of cloth that was already on his bed and began to wipe the sweat from his brow. She said to him, "You're going to be all right. Everything will be all right."

In the meantime, one of the doctors on duty found out about Maria from the old man she met when she entered the hospital. So the doctor went to talk to her about her brother's condition.

Patrick had had a fever for the past twenty-four hours, but the doctors were more concerned with the infection in his leg. The antibiotics didn't seem to be fighting the infection, and they were afraid it would spread throughout his entire body.

"Hello, young lady. I am Dr. David. I was told that you are Patrick's sister. Honestly, we didn't think any of his family members would come to visit because we know that Patrick is not from this region. But I am glad he has someone with him because later in the day, he's scheduled for surgery."

"Surgery? What kind of surgery?" asked Maria, concern in her tone.

"The antibiotics we gave him won't fight the infection in his leg, and he is at high risk. We need to amputate his leg as soon as possible," said the doctor.

"And then, will he be better?"

"To amputate his leg is our only option to stop the infection from spreading throughout his entire body. So we'll just have to wait and see. I can't promise anything."

Patrick was in surgery for almost three hours. Then, he was transferred to the recovery room for another two hours before he was moved back into his bed. But when he finally opened his eyes, he couldn't believe what he saw.

"Maria? Is that really you?" asked Patrick as he tried to lift his head to take a better look at the woman sitting by his bed, asleep on a chair.

Maria stood up from her chair as soon as she heard her name. When she saw her brother trying to sit up in his bed, she quickly put her right hand behind his head while her other hand reached for his left hand.

"How do you feel, brother?" she asked.

Patrick looked at his sister in disbelief, and his eyes began to flood with tears.

"I can't believe my eyes! Is that really you? How did you get all the way here in Bucharest?"

"Don't we share the same blood? What are families for if they are not there for you when you need them the most?" replied Maria with a smile on her face.

As Patrick listened to his sister, he tried to adjust himself and felt a sharp pain shoot up through what was left of his left leg. Unaware that his leg had been amputated, he reached under the sheet with his right hand to adjust his left leg, only to be horrified by the realization that something was not right. He slowly lifted the sheet, but before he could pull it off, Maria grasped his hand.

"Patrick, everything will be all right," she said to him.

Patrick knew something was wrong, so he pulled the sheet away from his legs. He was shocked to see that his left leg was missing. After lying motionless for a few moments, processing the situation, he finally said, "At least I am still alive. But it's so weird not having a leg when I can still feel it."

Patrick's surgery went well, but since he had to remain in the hospital for at least another week, Maria decided to visit Ms. Clara and her husband, Dr. Nicholas, in the meantime. She felt the need to check on them as well. Hopefully, nothing bad happened to them during the bombing, and then she could thank them again for everything they did for her on her last trip to Bucharest.

Their house was approximately a thirty-minute walk from the hospital, so Maria left the following day, first thing in the morning, eager to see them again. But upon arriving at Ms. Clara's home, it appeared like nobody was home.

Maria rang the bell a few more times, but since nobody answered the door, she decided to wait on the entryway stairs of their house for a little bit, just in case they might return home at any moment.

However, after almost an hour of waiting in front of their house, neither Ms. Clara nor Dr. Nicholas returned home. So Maria thought it was time to go back to the hospital.

"I will come again tomorrow," she said to herself as she stood up to leave.

Walking down the road, Maria started to recall memories from her last trip to Bucharest. She realized she was on a different route than the one she had taken from the hospital when she found herself behind a disarrayed line of people. They were waiting on the sidewalk and slowly entering a building, each holding a Bible. The building didn't look like a church, but since everyone was holding a bible, it seemed like it was a place where people met for conversation or to worship God.

Maria decided to enter the building as well to say some prayers for Patrick and the rest of her family. She got in the line behind an elderly lady.

"Good morning, young lady. Is this your first time here? I've never seen you here before," said the old lady.

"Good morning. Yes, this is my first time here. I somehow ended up here on my walk and saw this long line of people. If I hadn't seen everyone holding a Bible, I would not have realized that this was a place of worship," responded Maria.

"Oh, dear. Our church got destroyed by the air bombing, so we are blessed to be able to use this building every Sunday, where we can all get together to pray."

After entering the building, Maria took a seat in one of the available chairs at the back of the room, near the old lady. Stories were read from the Bible by a priest, and songs were sung out loud. At the end of the mass, when everybody stood up, Maria turned around toward the door, thinking that everyone would start walking outside, but she realized that everyone was walking the opposite way. The people walked down the aisle, turned left at the pulpit, and entered another room.

"Come on, dear. Please come and eat with us," said the old lady to Maria.

"Today, they are serving pasta and soup, and everyone is welcome," continued the old lady.

"I really appreciate your kindness, but I need to get going. Maybe some other time," replied Maria.

"By the way, my name is Maria, and it was a pleasure meeting you, Ms. . . . ?"

"Oh, it was a pleasure talking to you, Maria. My name is Margaret, and I hope that I will see you again."

"I hope so, too. And I have to say that I am very glad that I have found this place. I really needed to be surrounded by people who pray to God today," replied Maria.

"Young lady, you didn't find this place by chance. Always remember that everything in life happens for a reason," continued the old lady. Then she turned around and walked toward the room where the food was already being served.

Maria walked outside, and as she looked around to see which way she should go toward the hospital, a piece of paper blowing softly in the wind landed softly upon her ankle, then continued to tumble across the street where a bunch more of the same type of papers became trapped along the wall of the building.

Maria, remembering what the old lady just told her about everything in life happening for a reason, decided to run across the street to see what was written on the piece of paper. She grabbed one of the flyers from the wall and began to read it to herself.

"The theater is looking for someone to fill the costume designer position. Traveling around the country is required."

Maria felt it was just a matter of time before Patrick would be sent back home to Transylvania. She decided to apply for the costume designer position, hoping that traveling around the country might increase her chances of finding Maximus.

Therefore, before she headed back to the hospital, Maria stopped by the theater first, which was located in the heart of the city.

Luckily, the building was still standing after the city was nearly destroyed by bombs just a few days before, but as she tried to open the front door, it seemed as if it was locked. So she went to the side of the building to try to open the side door to get in. However, that door was locked as well, and there weren't any cars parked at the back of the building. But then, Maria saw a small doorbell on the side of the door, and she rang it.

She waited a few seconds and rang it again, but since nobody answered, she gave up and decided that she would come back later in the evening or the following day. But as soon as she turned to leave, the door suddenly opened.

"How may I help you, young lady?" asked an old man dressed in a black suit with a matching black hat.

"My name is Maria, and I am here for the costume designer position. Hopefully, it is still available," replied Maria as she handed him a flyer.

"Oh, I am just the doorman. Let me take you to the person who is in charge. Please come with me. My name is George."

After Maria stepped inside the building, the doorman locked the door behind her.

"Have you been here before?" asked the doorman.

"I have never been to a theater before."

"Then allow me to give you a quick tour before I take you to Mr. Peter," said the doorman as he began to describe its history.

"The theater was inaugurated on December 31, 1852, with the play *Zoe or the Borrowed Lover*. The building was built in the baroque style with 338 stalls on the main floor, three levels of lodges, a luxurious foyer with staircases of Carrara marble, and a large gallery in which students could attend free of charge. For its first two years, the theater was lit with tallow lamps. In 1854, these were replaced with rape oil lamps, then later with gas lights, and eventually, the theater transitioned to electric lightning."

After showing Maria the main lobby of the theater, George ended the tour on the center stage.

"Hello, George. Who do we have here?" said a man from the side of the stage.

"Sir, I was giving this young lady a tour of the theater. She is interested in the costume designer position," responded George.

"Then allow me to introduce myself. My name is Peter, and I am the artistic director of this theater. And you are?" asked Peter as he began approaching the stage.

Maria was in the center of the stage and felt like she was daydreaming with her eyes wide open. She never thought that she would have the opportunity to work in a theater, but lucky for her, after the tour of the theater with George and a conversation with Peter, Maria got the job as a costume designer.

"Well then, I will see you tomorrow so you can meet the entire stage crew as well as the actors," continued Peter before he left the stage, leaving Maria in the company of George.

"So what else could I say to you, young lady, other than congratulations and welcome to our theater!" exclaimed George, seeing the enthusiasm on Maria's face.

Maria was excited to get back to the hospital to share the news with her brother. After she thanked George for showing her the inside of the theater, she left and walked as fast as she could until she reached her brother's room, where she was surprised to see a large bouquet of lilies next to his bed.

"Wow, Patrick! Those are beautiful flowers. Someone must love you a lot to bring you that superb bouquet. Is there something I don't know?" asked Maria with a smile on her face.

"Yes, I do have someone who unquestionably loves me a lot, and you know her very well."

"I do?"

"Yes. That person is right here next to me. These flowers are for you, Maria," said Patrick.

"Yesterday was August 12. You were here to care for me, and we didn't celebrate you. Happy belated birthday," continued Patrick as he handed Maria the bouquet of flowers and sang her the birthday song. Soon, the song began to echo throughout the entire hospital as all the wounded soldiers in his room joined Patrick in singing "Happy Birthday" to his sister.

The day ended perfectly for Maria, and it seemed like the next day would be the same. Patrick looked much better than the day before, and Maria couldn't be happier with her new job because as soon as she arrived at the theater, she received a warm welcome and a hug from every one of them.

Most of the actors were young, with only a few being married, but they all seemed like a family, and Maria was thrilled to become part of it. With their help, she learned what she needed to prepare for their wardrobe for the big play scheduled for the grand opening that coming Sunday. Since she didn't need to create any new costumes for the actors, she was asked to watch their rehearsals to familiarize herself with the play.

Now, with her days filled by going back and forth between the hospital and the theater, time seemed to fly by, making it difficult for Maria to visit Ms. Clara's house again. Additionally, with her brother set to be released from the hospital and sent back home to Transylvania by train on the upcoming Wednesday, Maria also wanted to spend as much time as she could with him. So she was always in a hurry to leave right after the rehearsals.

George was the only person from the theater who knew about Maria's brother, so the day before the play, he pulled Maria aside after the rehearsals and asked her to bring her brother to watch the play.

"Just have him wait for me at the back door tomorrow evening by 7:50 p.m.," continued George as he winked at Maria.

Before the play began, George brought Patrick inside the theater through the back door and set up a chair for him at the side of the stage, where he could easily watch the performance.

After many long hours of rehearsal, the actors received a standing ovation from the audience. Those who wanted to socialize with the actors had the opportunity to do so in the lobby after the play. Maria did not feel comfortable joining the actors after the play since she had just started working for the theater, but Peter persuaded her to join everyone in the lobby.

"You need to be there as well, now that you are part of our family," Peter said to her.

Maria joined everyone in the lobby, but she knew Patrick was waiting for her, and she didn't want to spend too much time socializing. So when she thought nobody would notice, she tried to sneak away.

However, in her hurried state, she bumped into a woman and knocked the purse out of her hand.

"Oh, I apologize," said Maria sincerely while she quickly grabbed the purse off the floor.

"It's all right. You don't need to apologize," said the woman as she curiously studied Maria.

Maria handed the purse to the woman, and as their eyes met, they were stunned to see each other.

"Maria? Is that really you? Or are my eyes playing games with me?" asked the woman.

"Ms. Clara! I can't believe I am seeing you again. I am extremely happy to see that you are well, and I must say that you look amazing," said Maria.

"You look beautiful as well. And look at this pretty dress that you have on. Come on, let me see it better," continued Ms. Clara as she grabbed Maria by her hand and made Maria do a small twirl.

"And how is Mr. Nicholas?" asked Maria.

"Mr. Nicholas did not age a bit. He is still the same handsome man. What about you, Maria? What brought you back to Bucharest after nine years, especially during this time of war?"

Ms. Clara began to ask Maria several questions before she found out about her brother waiting for her behind the stage, so she invited Maria and her brother to spend the night at their house.

"And I will not take no for an answer," said Ms. Clara.

Furthermore, as they drove to Ms. Clara's house and Maria told them that Patrick would head home on Wednesday and she would stay in Bucharest for another two weeks before she began traveling with the theater, Dr. Nicholas invited them to stay in their house until they would leave Bucharest.

Maria and Patrick were both relieved to know they had somewhere to stay besides the hospital, and Ms. Clara was delighted to have them both in her home.

However, two days passed quickly, and it was already Wednesday morning, August 23, when Mr. Nicholas drove Patrick and Maria to the train station from where all of the wounded soldiers were sent back to their homes. Along the train tracks, many people wanted to show appreciation to the soldiers by offering food and drinks. After Maria helped her brother get onto the train, Patrick grabbed her hand, looked into her eyes, and said, "Are you really sure you don't want to come back home with me?" hoping his sister would change her mind.

"I'm sure, Patrick. One day, we will see each other again. But until then, take care of yourself," said Maria as she gave him a long hug before she jumped out.

"Oh! And one more thing. As soon as you get home, call Ms. Clara so I know that you arrived home safely," continued Maria.

"I will," said Patrick as the conductor pulled the train whistle, alerting the people that the train was ready to leave the station.

Chapter Twelve

In the meantime, the Red Army reached Romanian territory, and Madame Kolontay, Stalin's agent in Stockholm, presented a draft armistice agreement to the Romanians, which, given the military situation, seemed a generous offer.

The Soviets demanded that the German armies leave Romania within fifteen days, and they pledged to only pass through the northern territory as they pushed west toward Hungary and Germany. Moreover, they pledged not to take Bucharest and the south of the country, and they also offered to recognize Romanian claims to Hungarian-occupied Transylvania.

But since the prime minister of Romania, Ion Antonescu, prepared to defend Romania against the Soviets, he decided to immediately deploy nine elite divisions on the Focsani-Namoloasa-Galati line, hoping they could hold the Soviets until Romanian diplomats would send a Soviet proposal and the armistice would be signed.

Meanwhile, anti-fascist elements in Romania were already plotting with King Michael to remove the Antonescu regime and end the war. The German forces in Romania were too weak to pose a significant threat, and the king did not want to fight the Soviets practically alone.

However, when opposition leader Iuliu Maniu, who was the leader of the democratic opposition to a communist takeover, intercepted the telegram with details on the armistice, King Michael directly cooperated in a plot to arrest Prime Minister Ion Antonescu. Arresting him was not an easy task, seeing that there was still support within the army, so King Michael invited Prime Minister Antonescu to the Royal Palace, where he insisted that the Prime Minister immediately sign an unconditional surrender to the Soviets.

However, the prime minister argued that the armistice he was negotiating was preferable. In response to the king's proposal, he refused, stating, "Signing unconditional surrender to the Russians is like jumping out of a plane without a parachute."

His words made King Michael leave the room. After a discussion with his advisors, he returned to the room and told Prime Minister Antonescu, "From this second, you and your ministers are all dismissed." Soldiers loyal to the king then entered the room, arrested the prime minister, and locked him up in the walk-in safe. Then, communist agents working with the king handed the prime minister over to the Soviets.

Furthermore, on the evening of August 23, everyone who was listening to the radio was surprised by a solemn announcement when King Michael broadcasted a proclamation to the nation announcing a break of diplomatic relations with Germany and an armistice with the Allies. The king declared that Romania had joined the Red Army against the Germans and would mobilize all its forces to liberate northern Transylvania and declare a ceasefire.

However, the Red Army ignored the king's ceasefire and continued their offensive, swiftly breaking through the Romanian defensive line as most Romanian soldiers refused to fight. The sudden turn of events caught the German diplomatic and military representatives in Romania off guard. The Nazis refused to recognize the new Romanian government and decided to attack Bucharest in an attempt to suppress it.

The first skirmishes took place between German and Romanian troops the following day after the announcement, where the Germans were immediately forced to launch a bombing of Bucharest, destroying a good part of the Royal Palace.

King Michael sought refuge with the queen mother in Oltenia, a region located between the foothills of the Carpathian Mountains and the Danube River. Meanwhile, the Romanian army, having refused to fight the Russians, began engaging the Germans and made their best effort to hold the capital until the Red Army arrived.

The morning before the German bombing, Maria and Ms. Clara were out walking Ms. Clara's dog. Many people were outside, talking in small groups about the king's announcement from the night before, still in disbelief that the long and terrible war had come to an end. However, they were soon to be disappointed when, out of the blue, all the conversations were hushed by a peculiar sound coming from above.

As everyone gazed into the sky, they initially had to squint due to the sun. Once their eyes adjusted, they saw tiny gleaming dots moving in formation high above. It quickly became clear that the anticipated peace had not yet arrived.

The German garrison stationed in Bucharest, refusing to surrender, decided to fight the Romanian forces now loyal to the new government. So with only a few airplanes, the Germans began terrorizing the capital with an aerial attack, flying low, assuring that the damage behind them would be tremendous. Unfortunately, there wasn't any warning about the aerial attack for the people of Bucharest. The loud explosions that began to rip throughout the city forced people to return to their homes immediately.

Maria and Ms. Clara turned around and began running toward the house as fast as they could. But before they knew it, an explosion from across the street slammed both of them against the ground. Dismembered body parts and pieces of the earth began scattering all around them as Ms. Clara was stunned and still disoriented, lying on the ground.

"Ms. Clara? Ms. Clara?" shouted Maria as she inspected Ms. Clara for any injuries.

Ms. Clara couldn't hear anything because of the loud ringing in her ears, but Maria helped her up and grabbed her dog, and they quickly ran to the house. Once there, they went straight down to the basement.

Likewise, all the people were rushing to hide in the basements of their houses or their apartment buildings, if they were fortunate enough to have one. The others could only pray for their survival while stuck above ground.

More and more explosions could be heard in the distance, lighting up the city. Suddenly, a bomb exploded just outside Clara's house, causing the cellar walls to shake so violently that dried mortar from the bricks created a fine cloud of dust in the air, making it difficult for both of them to breathe.

"Ms. Clara! Are you all right?" asked Maria as she struggled to speak.

"Yes. What about you?" Ms. Clara asked through the handkerchief that she was using as a filter.

Through the broken basement window, the sound of a woman crying hysterically could be heard, along with the heart-rendering cries of a baby right in front of the house.

"Maria? Can you hear that?" asked Ms. Clara.

"Yes, I do. Someone is probably hurt outside," responded Maria as she ran up the basement stairs to go outside.

Maria opened the front door and saw a young woman lying on the sidewalk, holding a baby close to her chest.

Maria realized she needed Ms. Clara's help to bring them into the basement before another aerial attack. But as she turned back toward the house, Ms. Clara was already behind her.

"I'll grab the child while you help the woman," Ms. Clara told Maria as she went to pick up the baby.

Maria went to help the woman up from the ground and saw that her back and right arm appeared to be shredded open.

"Thank you for your kindness," said the young woman as she clutched onto Maria.

"I am happy that we could hear you, but let's get inside the house. We'll be safer there," responded Maria as they walked toward the front door of the house.

Meanwhile, Ms. Clara was already in the basement, trying her best to offer the baby some comfort. She was gently rocking the baby in her arms while quietly singing a soothing song.

"Thank you again for your kindness," the young woman said as Maria helped her sit on the couch that was along the wall across from the window.

"My name is Dana, and that's my daughter, Andrada. We live only a few blocks away. My husband is probably very worried about us," continued the young woman as she stood up to take her daughter.

"It's all right, Dana. I'll take care of your daughter right now so you can rest a bit," said Ms. Clara.

In the meantime, there were more explosions outside. Some sounded far away, and some sounded very close. And as the hours passed, fear started to grip the people that the German soldiers might begin invading their homes.

Soon, night took over the city, and Maria knew she couldn't be the only one who was famished, so she decided to take advantage of the lull between bombings to go to the kitchen and get some food and water. She grabbed one of the lit candles from the basement and headed toward the kitchen. But as she reached the top of the stairs, she was startled by the sound of footsteps in the back hallway slowly coming her way.

Maria blew out the candle and quickly sneaked into the kitchen, finding her way to the drawer where Ms. Clara kept the knives. She tried to open the drawer quietly, but the kitchen cutlery made a noise.

"Clara? Is that you?" asked a male voice from the obscure hallway.

"No. It's me, Maria," responded Maria calmly once she realized the man's voice was Dr. Nicholas, Ms. Clara's husband.

"What are you doing in the dark in the kitchen? Is everything all right? Where is Clara?" asked Dr. Nicholas.

"Everything is all right, Dr. Nicholas. Ms. Clara is in the basement caring for a baby and the injured mother," answered Maria as she lit the candle with a match she had in the pocket of her dress.

Nicholas grabbed his first aid kit, and after Maria gathered some food and water, they both went down to the basement.

When Ms. Clara heard more than one set of footsteps coming down the stairs, she held the baby nervously as she waited to see who would appear on the staircase.

"Oh, thank God you are all right," said Ms. Clara with relief in her tone once she saw her husband.

Then, she put the sleeping baby next to her mother on the couch so she could hug and kiss her husband.

"I was worried sick about you," said Ms. Clara.

But before she could hug her husband again, the baby began to cry.

"I can take care of her, Dana," said Maria as she reached for the baby.

"Oh, it's all right, Maria. I will take care of her now. I feel much better," Dana said as she went to pick up her baby, only to realize that her body was still very weak from her injuries, and she couldn't lift her.

"Hi. My name is Dr. Nicholas, and I understand your name is Dana. You sound as if you are in pain. Please let Maria hold your baby for now, and with your permission, I would like to examine your injuries."

Dr. Nicholas sat in a chair next to Dana, and as he took her wrist to check her pulse, he noticed some injuries.

"Your arm and back are badly injured. Is there anything else that hurts?" asked Dr. Nicholas as he fished for his pen torch from his bag to shine it in her eyes and test her pupils' reflexes.

"My right shoulder and the right side of my back hurt the most," answered Dana.

Carefully, Dr. Nicholas started cleansing Dana's wounds, but as he pressed on her ribs, Dana gasped.

"Oh, sorry," said Dr. Nicholas.

"Can you lift your right arm for a second, please?" he continued.

Once he finished the examination, he sat back in the chair and began to explain the injuries she sustained.

"Physically, you have a couple of broken ribs, a minor dislocation of your shoulder, and some bruising and lacerations. So I think we should consider going to the hospital as soon as it is safe to leave our house," said Dr. Nicholas.

The bombing seemed to be over in the morning, so Dr. Nicholas decided to take Dana and Maria to the hospital to receive better care while Clara would stay home with the baby. And since Dana's house was nearby, he decided to take the road that passed her house to check on her husband.

"Dana, stay with Maria inside the car while I look to see if your husband is inside," said Dr. Nicholas as he parked the car right in front of the fifth house on the street where Dana said she lived.

Nicholas got out of the car, and as he looked at the house through the dense shrubs that hid the house from the main street, the house seemed undamaged. Thus, he climbed the stairs and rang the doorbell. He waited a few seconds, but no one answered, so he decided to ring the bell again two more times.

Thinking Dana's husband wasn't there, he decided to go back to the car, but as he turned to leave, he caught a glimpse of the curtains moving.

"Someone must be inside the house. But why wouldn't they answer the door?" Dr. Nicholas thought to himself.

Just as Dr. Nicholas was ready to ring the bell again, he was startled when the front door swung wide open, and inside stood an angry man.

"Who the hell are you, and why are you ringing my bell so many times?" said the man aggressively, with the smell of alcohol on his breath.

This man appeared to have had a hard, long night. His white shirt was stained and torn with some blood spots, his gray trousers were ripped at the knees, and his face showed pain and fatigue.

"Are you Luka? Are you Dana's husband?" Dr. Nicholas asked.

The second the man heard Dana's name, he became more aggressive.

"What do you know about my wife?" shouted the man in frustration as he grabbed Dr. Nicholas by his shirt and shook him.

The man could be easily heard from the car, and Dana recognized that voice right away.

"That's my husband! Please help me get out of the car to see him," said Dana.

Dana began calling her husband's name, and you could hear the pain in her voice from her broken ribs.

Maria opened the car door, and when Dana's voice caught Luka's attention, he instantly stopped yelling at

Dr. Nicholas. Luka turned around, and he could see Dana slowly walking toward him as she held onto a young woman that he didn't recognize.

"Oh, thank God you are alive!" exclaimed Luka as he ran toward her.

But when he saw Dana's teary eyes, he didn't know they were tears of joy. His voice started to crack as he asked Dana about their daughter since she wasn't there.

"Luka!" interrupted Dr. Nicholas.

"My name is Dr. Nicholas, and we need to take your wife to the hospital as soon as possible. Your daughter is safe and in very good hands. My wife is taking care of her at our house, which is right around the corner. Come on! Let's all get back inside the car, and we can talk on the way to the hospital," continued Dr. Nicholas.

The hospital was approximately ten miles away from Dana's house, which gave Luka the opportunity to explain to Dana that last night, he had been out searching for them all night long. Consequently, he returned home only with built-up frustration and fear from not finding his wife and daughter. His only escape from his pain and sorrow was to drown himself in alcohol right before Dr. Nicholas rang the bell.

On their way to the hospital, people could be seen trying to salvage as many personal belongings as they could from what remained inside their houses. Others were simply holding hands with their children and crying as they stared at their homes in disbelief at how they had become ruins overnight.

Once they arrived at the hospital, Dr. Nicholas parked the car as close as possible to the entrance. After Luka helped his wife get out of the car, they all headed up the ramp toward the emergency room.

At the entrance, two women were waiting to help and direct people to the areas they needed, as each floor of the hospital was set up for different types of injuries.

"What happened to the young woman?" asked one of the ladies.

"She has broken ribs, a minor shoulder dislocation, and some bruising and lacerations," responded Dr. Nicholas.

"All right. Take her all the way to the end of this hallway. Then, at the end of this hallway, you'll see a door, and you need to wait outside until someone calls you inside," explained the woman as she pointed toward the end of the hallway.

The hallway was already packed with people who had missing limbs or major burns. Some people who didn't have any injuries were there with photos of their family members, asking if anyone had seen them.

Despite nurses and doctors trying to help as many patients as quickly as they could, it still took an hour before a nurse called Dana into the examination room to be seen by a doctor.

"Please, sit on the table so I can examine your wounds," the doctor directed Dana.

After Luka helped Dana onto the table, the doctor cut off part of her bloodied dress to assess the extent of her injuries.

"My apologies. I will try to make this as comfortable as possible," said the doctor as he saw Dana wince a little because her dress had become stuck to the dried blood.

"Well, it appears as though you have sustained quite a few cuts and bruises. I just need to place some stitches on your wounds, and that will aid in your healing."

Then, as the doctor examined Dana's back and chest area, he noticed her jaw clamped tightly, and she inhaled sharply, indicating that she was in pain.

"I will also need to bandage your rib cage because a couple of ribs are broken. After that, it will be a matter of time until they heal," explained the doctor as he finished the exam.

The hospital was too crowded at that time for Dana to be admitted overnight, so the doctor decided to send her home.

"Besides, you'll get better rest at home. But you'll have to come back in about two weeks so I can make sure everything is healing properly," stated the doctor.

Dana and Luka thanked the doctor and returned to the waiting area, where Dr. Nicholas and Maria were waiting for them.

"How's everything?" asked Dr. Nicholas.

"The doctor said Dana should get better, but I need to bring her back to the hospital in two weeks to check if she is healing."

"That sounds good. And you don't need to worry about anything in the meantime. I will be happy to check on Dana's recovery every day until you bring her back to the hospital."

Therefore, they all headed back to Dr. Nicholas's house so Dana and Luka could pick up their daughter. Unexpectedly, as they were only a few blocks away from the hospital, a German airplane flying low started dropping bombs just a few blocks away from them. The fright of what would happen next forced Dr. Nicholas to speed up to get to the house as fast as he could.

The area quickly became smothered in smoke, and as they were passing near the theater, Maria noticed a large plume of dark smoke coming from the front entrance.

"Oh no, the theater just got hit! Please pull over, Dr. Nicholas. I am getting out!" yelled Maria.

"Maria! There is nothing you can do. Let's go home!" said Dr. Nicholas.

"But I need to see what's going on. Please, Dr. Nicholas, pull over!" shouted Maria.

The moment Dr. Nicholas stopped the car, Maria opened the door and hopped out.

"I will see you back at the house!" exclaimed Maria as she ran toward the side entrance of the theater.

Surprisingly, the door was wide open, and Maria could see a man rushing out of the theater while carrying a big pile of garments. The man dropped the clothing on top of another pile of clothes that had been thrown on the ground, further away from the building, and quickly turned around to go back inside. Only then did Maria realize the man was George, the doorman.

"George! What are you doing?" she yelled at him.

"I need to get one more thing!" answered George, who was in a hurry to get back inside the theater.

"George, it's not safe to go back inside!" shouted Maria as she grabbed his hand, worried about what could happen to him.

George started working for the theater as a doorman at a young age, and the only family he knew were the actors he saw every day. His late wife, the only woman George ever loved, was an actress in this theater. Sadly, she died in 1930 in her sleep, sending George into a great depression. As a result, George decided to quit the job and seek a different way to live. Yet, nothing could heal the wound of losing the love of his life except drinking every night until he passed out in strange places.

But with help from the actors, who were already family, George was brought back to the theater to slowly get back on his feet. He was offered one of the back rooms inside the theater as his personal space to live in, and that was the best thing that happened to him since he lost his wife.

George was inside the theater when the front of the building got hit by a German plane, and he knew right away it was only a matter of time until the entire building would be under fire. So he decided that before he would save himself, he would try to save as many costumes as he could. The costumes were kept in a room behind the main stage, and thanks to George's courage and quick reaction, the costumes were saved before the entire theater caught on fire.

However, when George wanted to go back inside to retrieve something important from his room, Maria tried to stop him, believing it was too dangerous. However,

Undeterred and fearless, George rushed back into the theater, willing to risk his life for whatever he needed to save.

The flames had grown at a marvelous speed, and the entire entrance of the theater was already engulfed by flames. The visibility was reduced to zero, and the fire had taken over the main stage before George got to his room. However, since he was very familiar with the theater, he could still quickly retrieve what he wanted, and by the time the thick smoke had already spread through the entire theater, George made it out of the building.

"What did you need to go back for, George? You could have died in there."

"Soon, the theater will be in ashes, and the only connection to my wife will be lost forever. So I needed to go back to save the only photograph I have of her, even if I died trying," replied George as he pulled out his wife's photograph from his shirt pocket and handed it to Maria.

The flames and smoke began to billow up into the sky through the roof of the theater.

"George! Come with me!" shouted Maria as she grabbed George's hand to walk him away from the theater.

Maria walked George across the street, and then, as fast as she could, she started moving the pile of clothes that George saved and brought them over.

One pile at a time, Maria saved them again before they could burn from the fire, but eventually, they would need to figure out what to do with the theater wardrobe.

Until then, all they could do was sit next to each other and watch in horror as the theater burned to the ground.

"Do you guys need some help with the costumes?" said a woman unexpectedly from behind them.

Maria and George turned around at the same time to see a beautiful lady with a slender build, long flowing white hair cascading over her shoulders, and a pair of mesmerizing emerald-green eyes. She waited for them to answer as she stood at the front entrance of the building behind Maria and George.

The lady's eyes looked a little sad, but as soon as George made eye contact with her, her face lit up right away.

"If you would like, you are welcome to bring all those costumes inside my apartment," continued the lady.

Apparently, the woman was living on the second floor of the building that faced the theater, and she witnessed Maria and George move the clothes in front of her building.

"Oh, thank you very much. It is very kind of you to help two strangers," replied George.

"I might be a stranger to you, but you are absolutely not a stranger to me. I have seen you many times around the theater, and I know that you have been working for the theater for many, many years. My name is Marcela."

"It is a pleasure, Marcela. I am George, and this is Maria," said George.

Meanwhile, as two fire trucks from the closest fire station parked by the theater and the firefighters began doing their best to put the fire out, Maria, George, and

Marcela grabbed as many costumes as they could and followed Marcela up the stairs to her apartment.

They put the costumes in the wide hallway at the entrance of Marcela's apartment. Before heading back out for the remaining costumes, Maria insisted that George and Marcela stay in the apartment while she went to retrieve the rest.

"Then, I will make some tea for everyone," said Marcela.

"And, George, you don't have to wait in the hallway. Come in and feel free to take a seat on the couch while I prepare the tea," she continued.

Marcela's apartment had two large bedrooms and had a warm and inviting feeling. She didn't have much metal or glass throughout her apartment; almost everything was made from wood, including her furniture, and the windows had long curtains. It looked as if she liked her apartment as clean and neat as possible, and everything looked perfect.

By the time Maria went back upstairs with the last pile of clothing, the chamomile tea that Marcela had prepared for everyone was ready. They sat down at the dining room table with their tea, and time passed quickly while they got to know each other. Before they knew it, it was already late at night.

"Oh, I can't believe it's already ten o'clock. I need to get going. Dr. Nicholas and Ms. Clara may be worried about me," exclaimed Maria, getting up from her chair.

"You're right, Maria. We should both get going," replied George as he stood up.

Marcela didn't want to send them out into the dangerous night, offering them the opportunity to remain in her apartment for the remainder of the night.

George, who had just lost his home to the fire, was extremely grateful for Marcela's offer. However, Maria decided to leave Marcela's apartment and return to Ms. Clara and Dr. Nicholas's home, planning to come back to the theater the next day.

The following morning, Maria got up early to go back to the theater. But before she even opened the front door of the house, she could hear Ms. Clara from the kitchen.

"Maria? Is that you?" asked Ms. Clara as she stuck her head out through the kitchen, looking for Maria.

"Let me make you some breakfast before you leave. Last night, you didn't want to eat anything before bed, so you have to be starving. And while you eat, maybe you can tell me more about what happened at the theater."

Maria began to share every detail of what had happened at the theater the day before. Meanwhile, Ms. Clara was cooking two scrambled eggs with two pieces of sausage. But as soon as Maria finished eating breakfast, she thanked Ms. Clara for the food and left in a hurry to get to the theater.

Once Maria arrived back at the theater, it was still hard for her to comprehend the reality of the situation. But she wasn't alone in her disbelief; she noticed George standing by the window of Marcela's apartment, staring in shock at the remnants of the theater.

Maria started waving at him, but it didn't seem like George saw her. She continued waving, hoping he would eventually see her. However, George was lost in thought, reminiscing about his wife and the time they had spent together in the theater, too absorbed in his daydream to notice Maria.

"George? Isn't that Maria?" asked Marcela as she appeared in the window next to George and noticed Maria outside waving.

"Yes, that's Maria," replied George as Marcela opened the window.

"Good morning, Maria! Would you like to come upstairs?" shouted Marcela.

"No, thank you. I'll stay here for now."

"Then we're coming outside as well," replied Marcela.

While George, Marcela, and Maria met and began talking with each other, the actors unexpectedly began to show up one after another. Each actor was heartbroken when they saw that the theater had become another victim of the war. But when they learned that the costumes were saved by George, it gave them hope.

However, given the changing situation in the country—with the Red Army entering Bucharest on August 31, the Romanian government quickly placing its armed forces under Soviet command, and a Soviet puppet government being installed shortly thereafter— the actors decided to wait and see the outcome of this big change before resuming their performances.

At that moment, without a formal armistice, Soviet troops treated the Romanians as a hostile force. Following King Michael's ceasefire order, between 114,000 and 160,000 Romanian soldiers surrendered to the Soviets without resistance. These soldiers were forced to march to remote detention camps in the Soviet Union, with approximately a third of them tragically dying along the way.

Moreover, when an armistice was signed on September 12, 1944, surrendering to the Soviets and other Allies, Romania was obliged to provide at least twelve infantry divisions to fight alongside Soviet forces. In reality, Romania provided significantly more than twelve divisions, possibly the equivalent of twenty divisions, to assist the Red Army in expelling the Germans from Romanian territory and from Hungary and Czechoslovakia. During these campaigns, Romania contributed the fourth-largest Allied force in Europe, after the Soviet Union, the United States, and Great Britain.

Chapter Thirteen

By the time the armistice was signed on September 12, 1944, surrendering to the Soviets and the Allies, Patrick should have already been home, as he had left Bucharest almost three weeks earlier. However, he was nowhere to be found, and with no word from him, Maria and her parents grew increasingly concerned. What they did not know was that on the night of August 23, when Romania switched sides to join the Red Army, Patrick's train was just 45 miles from the Transylvanian border, which had already been invaded by the Red Army. Despite King Michael's ceasefire, the Russians continued to capture Romanians and transport them to detention camps in Russia.

Patrick and other wounded Romanian soldiers were just beginning to learn about the latest news of the war when they were abruptly awakened by the screeching noise of the train brakes. The train had come to a halt, and loud Russian voices could be heard outside.

Patrick peeked through a crack in the wooden planks of the train wall near his head and saw that they were in the middle of a forested mountainous area. All he could make out was a dense expanse of wilderness and a large group of Russian soldiers.

"Everybody, get off the train! Now! Move it!" yelled the Russian soldiers with their rifles pointing toward the wounded Romanian soldiers, who were doing their best to exit the train depending on the severity of their injuries.

Suddenly, the sound of an approaching airplane added to the terror that the confused and wounded Romanian soldiers were experiencing.

"Hurry up! Move faster!" the Russian soldiers continued to yell at the wounded Romanian soldiers.

But before everyone could get out, two German planes appeared overhead, flying low, and bullets began to pierce through everyone and everything, forcing everyone to seek cover.

At that time, German and Hungarian forces had already launched an attack on the Romanians from inside the Northern Transylvanian border, occupying a strategic position just 15 miles south of the Transylvanian frontier. This was 30 miles away from where Patrick's train was. The German forces had already gained control of the railway stations and important intersections. Since the Germans were attempting to advance further south, Patrick and the other wounded Romanian soldiers found themselves caught in the middle of the battle.

As a result, the unexpected situation caused the wounded Romanian soldiers to scramble desperately from the train in an attempt to save themselves by taking cover underneath it. Some of them were fortunate enough to jump safely, while others were shot and killed as they made their escape.

Without warning, another plane roared overhead, and the sound of bullets hitting the ground and smashing into the rail cars filled the air.

Patrick tried to quickly position himself on one leg while preparing his crutches to aid his escape from the train when someone pushed him from behind, causing him to lose his balance and fall flat on the ground.

"Patrick! Quick, give me your hand!" shouted someone from beneath the train.

Patrick turned his head and saw Eugene, also a discharged Romanian soldier who had been injured on the same night as Patrick. That night, Eugene had completely lost vision in his right eye and had a large cut across his right cheek. He also had a severe shoulder injury that affected his mobility and only allowed him to move his arm from the elbow.

Patrick and Eugene had met when they boarded the train in Bucharest, and they quickly became friends as they stood next to each other, exchanging stories.

"Hurry, Patrick!" continued Eugene as he pulled Patrick underneath the train, where they took cover as close to the ground as possible.

The loud sound of the German planes above them, combined with the sound of the Russian guns firing back rapidly, was absolutely terrifying.

Suddenly, an explosion erupted behind them, followed shortly by another explosion. Black smoke began rising from the trees, and the burning tail of a plane could be seen. A few seconds later, the second plane went down.

"What now?" asked Patrick.

"We have to go. Now is the time," responded Eugene.

While Patrick reached for his crutches, Eugene grabbed two rifles from dead Russian soldiers.

"Let's go!" shouted Eugene.

They crawled toward the forest and, once they felt safe, stood up and hurried away from the battlefield. When they reached one of the German planes that had crashed into the forest, they saw that the fuselage had burned completely away from the frame. The burned body of the pilot was still seated in the cockpit, with his arms resting on the edge of the frame as if he had been trying to pull himself out. His legs were likely pinned beneath the twisted wreckage.

"Eugene, I need to rest for a while. My leg is killing me," said Patrick.

Walking with crutches on the rough terrain exhausted Patrick quickly.

"All right. Let's get some rest for a few minutes, but we'll have to keep going, Patrick. We need to find a place to hide before sunrise."

Not long after they started moving again, heavy raindrops began to fall fast, and the ground beneath their feet grew slick. Their clothes got soaked, and as the wind grew stronger, the heavy rain stung their faces and interfered with their vision, making it difficult to see where their steps would land on the dangerous terrain.

"I think it's time to find shelter!" Eugene shouted, noticing that Patrick was struggling with his crutches on the soggy earth.

They stopped and looked around for a moment, but because nothing looked like shelter, they had to continue to fight their way through the pouring rain for another half an hour before the sun started to peek above the horizon.

As they approached a small waterfall, they noticed an opening in the mountain that seemed like a potential shelter. They hurried to explore it and were surprised to find that it was a spacious cave that extended much deeper into the mountain than its entrance had suggested.

"This is it! This cave will be our shelter," Patrick exclaimed happily, knowing he could finally rest. He sat down on the cold ground, stretched out, and soon fell asleep for hours. Meanwhile, Eugene ventured out of the cave to gather some wood to make a fire. He returned with some sticks and dry brush and used rocks from inside the cave to create a fire pit.

After trying several times, Eugene finally managed to start a small fire. Once it was going well, he went back outside to gather more firewood as rain poured and the wind howled through the cave.

All at once, a loud crack of thunder shook the mountain so violently that the crackling sound rattled Patrick. Unaware that he had been sleeping for hours, he awoke shouting, "Take cover! Take cover!"

But the brief silence that followed encouraged him to take a look around and find that he was safe in the cave with a warm fire by his side.

"I made a fire while you were resting," said Eugene as he threw more wood on the fire.

Patrick was cold, but thanks to Eugene, he wasn't chilled to the bone. So he braced himself with trembling arms to get up, mentally commanding his leg not to fold beneath him.

His belly started to rumble, and for the first time in over a day, Patrick's thoughts turned to food as he watched the fire. He closed his eyes and could easily picture his favorite dinner of stuffed cabbage with pork meat and homemade fresh bread that he usually had on a Sunday evening with his entire family. The only thing Patrick had since he departed Bucharest was water.

Lucky for him, Eugene came across some berry bushes while gathering some wood for the fire.

"There you go. I have something for you," said Eugene as he took some berries out of his coat pocket and handed them to Patrick, who quickly stuffed them into his mouth.

Berries were not what Patrick craved, but they would have to suffice until morning. He woke up to his stomach rumbling again while Eugene was still asleep. Noticing that the rain had stopped, Patrick added some more wood to the fire and decided to search for food.

Patrick knew they were by the river, and the river had fish. Catching fish was something that he could do. He had always been good at it, but he was used to using a fishing pole and bait. However, as he was walking toward the water, he noticed a large rabbit hopping into a hole. The rabbit must have heard him approaching and darted back into the burrow.

Patrick undid his belt and, after he shaped a noose, carefully walked to the rear of the hole and settled down quietly on his stomach to wait.

Twenty minutes passed like an eternity when Patrick could finally see the twitching nose poking out through the noose. Soon, the nose was followed by its little hairy head and two stumpy ears, shivering apprehensively. The moment the rabbit hopped over the bottom of the noose with its front legs, Patrick closed the noose around the rabbit's waist with a quick jerk of the belt.

However, the rabbit struggled to free itself and nearly succeeded. It got one of its front paws loose, but before the rabbit escaped, Patrick grabbed the back of its neck and snapped it. Then, he released the rabbit from the noose, retied his belt around his waist, and returned to the cave.

"Eugene! It's a glorious day!" he exclaimed as he entered the cave, carrying the dead rabbit around his neck.

Eugene opened his eyes and couldn't believe what he saw. Patrick was waving the dead rabbit in his hand like a trophy.

"Let's go by the river to get our breakfast ready," continued Patrick.

Once they arrived by the water, Eugene pulled out his flint knife from his pocket and started skinning the rabbit.

"Patrick! I have to say, it is a glorious day indeed. Look at all these fish in the river," exclaimed Eugene.

"After you're done skinning the rabbit, let me have its skin and your knife. I have an idea," said Patrick.

Once Eugene was done skinning the rabbit, he handed the knife and the rabbit's skin to Patrick, who was sitting down on a rock by the stream while holding his crutches on his lap.

Patrick cut the rabbit skin into thin layers, which he used to tie the knife to the bottom of a crutch. Then, he took off his boot and rolled his pants to his knee before he made his way to a spot in the stream. He kept his balance using one crutch while the other crutch was ready to spear one of the three fish that began swimming around him.

Rapidly, he pounced like a cat. However, he not only missed the fish, but he also lost his balance and fell into the water. As he crawled out of the water, he saw Eugene smiling at him. Patrick began to smile back, and soon, they were both laughing out loud.

"Let me try it!" said Eugene as he started taking off his boots and rolling up his pants above his knees.

Patrick handed him the crutch with the knife tied to it, and it was Eugene's turn to wait patiently in the water.

Soon, a fish appeared, and Eugene tried his best to pierce the fish.

"I got the fish!" exclaimed Eugene happily as he raised the crutch from the water. He realized with embarrassment that he did not catch anything.

The fish, dazed and swimming erratically, was an easy target. Eugene tried to scoop it out of the stream with his hand but lost his balance and fell in. When he got back on his feet, he triumphantly held the fish in his hand.

"I can't believe I got it!" he yelled.

"For now, we should be all right with this fish and the rabbit. Let's just get back to the cave to cook them," continued Eugene.

The fresh food, clean water, and comfortable beds Patrick and Eugene made from leafy branches made their days easier. Ironically, these comforts also made it harder for them to decide when to leave. Despite the safety and comfort of the cave, they knew they needed to return to their families.

A few weeks later, without knowing the current state of the country, they decided to leave the cave at dawn. They walked cautiously along the river, hoping to find a village where they could gather information about the war. However, after hours of walking under the blazing sun, they had yet to encounter any villages or people.

"We should rest for a moment," said Eugene, as he noticed Patrick's face was bright red and full of sweat.

"I'm fine. We should keep walking."

"You are not fine, and this looks like a good place to rest. Let's sit here for a moment," insisted Eugene.

"But only for a little bit," replied Patrick as he sat down by the river with his crutches and his rifle next to him.

Patrick stretched out his leg, took his boot off, wiggled his toes, and plunged them into the water.

"Ah! This feels amazing!" sighed Patrick, and with his foot in the water, he lay back and closed his eyes. Exhaustion caused him to drift into a childhood memory, dreaming of fishing trips with his sister Maria. Meanwhile, Eugene leaned his rifle against a tree trunk and lay down to rest. Suddenly, he heard a noise coming from somewhere between the trees nearby.

"Patrick! Wake up!" whispered Eugene as he quickly grabbed his rifle.

Patrick opened his eyes and saw Eugene on alert and holding his rifle.

"Stay still," whispered Eugene as all of his senses were focused on what was coming toward them.

Patrick sat quietly for a dozen heartbeats before putting his boot back on. He then slowly crawled over to Eugene, and together, they tried to hide behind the tree.

"What's going on?" asked Patrick.

"I heard something."

They slowly began to stand up, shielding their eyes from the sunlight as they peered through the trees to investigate the sound Eugene had heard. They remained still but, unable to determine what was happening, began to inch forward toward the source of the noise.

Suddenly, dogs began to bark.

"I hope they are not Nazi dogs," whispered Eugene.

"But if they are, I am ready," responded Patrick.

As Patrick readied his rifle, he was surprised when he saw a herd of sheep. They were grazing next to a shepherd who was carrying a child on his shoulders, and two barefoot children were playing next to him with two mastiff dogs.

"Thank God. It's just a flock of sheep," said Patrick once he realized that there wasn't any danger coming their way.

When the children saw the two soldiers with rifles, they ran and hid behind a tree while the dogs barked and growled. The shepherd, noticing that the soldiers were wearing Romanian uniforms, gave a sharp whistle to quiet the dogs.

"What are you doing here in the middle of nowhere?" inquired the shepherd as he put the child down.

With a very smooth move, he reached behind him to his waist, where he felt for his gun, waiting to hear if the soldiers spoke Romanian.

"We mean no harm. We were just looking for a place to rest," responded Patrick.

The moment Romanian words came out of Patrick's mouth, the shepherd was no longer worried.

"Children! You heard the Romanian soldiers. You can come out now," the shepherd called.

"I can see that you are both wounded, and it seems like you are lost. So listen—my children and I are on our way back to our farm. It's about half an hour from here, and you are welcome to come with us. And in the meantime, you can tell me how you ended up here," continued the shepherd.

While they walked to the shepherd's farm, Patrick and Eugene shared their story and how they came to meet the shepherd in the forest. Then, the shepherd told them that the Red Army was fighting to occupy Transylvania as they spoke.

Consequently, it sounded like it was a matter of time until Patrick and Eugene could cross the border and return home safely.

Chapter Fourteen

Back in Bucharest, after the theater burned to the ground, the actors decided to start performing only around the city during the war. After that, they would consider traveling all around the country to perform. In the meantime, since they relied upon donations from the public until they could perform on the improvised stage that was built in the empty parking lot at the back of the theater by volunteers, it was important for them to perform anywhere that a large crowd could gather to watch their performances.

The actors only performed their latest play since they did not have the time and place to learn a new play. However, at the same time, performing again and again made the play better.

Maria continued to stay with Ms. Clara and Dr. Nicholas in Bucharest. It was a great relief for her to have a warm and beautiful place to rest after her long, busy days helping the actors. Every night, as she returned to Ms. Clara's home, Maria hoped to hear good news about Patrick.

As summer turned to fall, by October 25, Soviet and Romanian troops had succeeded in driving out the Hungarians and German troops from northern Transylvania. After many prayers, Maria received the long-awaited news about her brother Patrick on the evening of October 27.

"Patrick is home safely!" shouted Ms. Clara as soon as Maria entered the house after another special performance that was organized for the Red Army.

The good news gave Maria hope, and as the actors gathered enough money for travel expenses and planned their itinerary, Maria looked forward to happier days with the theater.

The actors made plans for the length of stay in each region and city, and to ensure that everything was meticulously organized, they hired someone to scout accommodations and arrange transportation for each destination.

After three weeks of planning, two actors unexpectedly decided against the journey due to mixed emotions about leaving their families behind during an uncertain time. The journey had to be postponed in order for the theatrical group to find two replacements. But with everybody's help, two semi-professional actors got hired to play their parts, and three weeks later, their journey began.

The actors learned how to make choices quickly, how to be self-sufficient and reliable, and how to tackle whatever parts they were handed. And when they weren't on stage, there was always a script to rehearse. The theaters were sold out for every performance, and in larger cities, the actors often had to perform twice a day. Despite the demanding schedule, the actors stayed energized by the joy they saw on the audience's faces.

However, moving from one area to another created as much of an emotional journey as a physical one, and many actors began to experience homesickness at some point. Some actors wanted to leave several times to return home, while others felt pangs of homesickness but didn't complain because they knew they made the decision to be there.

Days turned into weeks, weeks turned into months, and months turned into years. By mid-October of 1946, the actors had completed their entire itinerary. Even though their journey together was fantastic, it was time for them to return to Bucharest.

Maria was disappointed that she couldn't find Maximus. During each play, she scanned the audience, praying to see her lost love. But as strong as she was, she accepted that her husband had not been found yet. Seeing no point in agonizing over a future in the capital without him, she decided it was time for her to go back home to Transylvania and resume her life.

Her decision to leave surprised all the actors, especially since they had not been apart for four years, making their separation difficult. Nonetheless, Maria booked a late-afternoon train to Transylvania for the same day they arrived in Bucharest, and the actors decided to wait with her. However, as the train pulled into the station, Maria began to feel troubled about leaving the theater. She worried that leaving might reduce her chances of finding Maximus.

However, after a few minutes of silence, she accepted what she wanted to do. As she pulled out Maximus's dog tags from underneath her shirt, she kissed them with tears in her eyes and said quietly, "For now, let's just go home, my love."

Suddenly, a loud horn gave a warning that the train was ready to depart. Maria hugged and kissed everyone before getting on the train. She quickly maneuvered through the crowd of people and made her way to the end of the train. She found an empty seat, stowed her luggage, and was instantly joined by a kind-looking woman who settled herself across the table. The lady wore a tweed coat with a Cairngorm brooch on the lapel and a green fur hat.

As their eyes met from across the table, Maria smiled politely.

"Oh, my! What a cold day. While I waited for the train, my feet became ice-cold. But at least it's not raining. Anything is better than rain, I always say. My name is Delia," she said as she smiled in return.

"My name is Maria."

The train shuddered and screeched, and soon, they were speeding away. Maria grabbed Maximus's dog tags and tried to relax after a long day when the lady began talking to Maria again.

"So, Maria, where are you traveling?"

"I am going back home to Transylvania," responded Maria as she put Maximus's dog tags back inside of her shirt.

"Where in Transylvania?"

"To a small village outside of Cluj-Napoca."

"Then, my dear, we will have to keep each other company because I am going to Cluj-Napoca as well."

As time passed, Maria and Delia got to know each other. As they talked about their families, their homes, and their lives across the country, Maria could not believe it when Delia told her she was working for the theater in Cluj-Napoca.

"Why is it so hard to believe?" asked Delia.

"Oh, it's not that I do not believe you. It's just such a big coincidence that you are working for the theater. I have also worked for a theater, the one in Bucharest. I have just returned from—"

"Then you must know Peter," interrupted Delia.

"Of course, I know him. He is the person who hired me and gave me the opportunity to work with wonderful actors. But how do you know Mr. Peter?"

"I used to perform for twenty years on the same stage with my husband at the Cluj-Napoca Theater. But after a tragic car accident that killed him, I couldn't perform any longer. But now, I have the same job as Peter. I am the artistic director for the Cluj-Napoca Theater. Peter and I just met the other day for dinner to discuss a collaboration between theaters."

"But if you don't mind me asking, why did you stop working for the theater?" continued Delia.

"Actually, today was my last day working there. Mr. Peter hired me as the dressmaker back in August 1944, right before the theater was bombed by the Germans. Since then, the actors and I have been on the journey of a lifetime. We just returned from—"

"So you are Maria, the costume designer that Peter told me about. I would love to hear more about you," interrupted Delia again with a sweet smile on her face.

Maria happily answered questions that Delia asked her, but slowly, without realizing it, they both drifted off to sleep.

The moment Maria opened her eyes, she saw the sun shining. It was a beautiful morning with not a single cloud in the sky. She realized the train was only minutes away from the Cluj-Napoca station, and her excitement caused a smile to form on her face as she thought about seeing her family soon.

Delia was still asleep, but as soon as the conductor pulled the horn to announce their arrival at the station, her eyes opened instantly.

"Did we already arrive in Cluj-Napoca, Maria?" she asked.

"Yes," answered Maria, standing by the window in the hopes of catching sight of her family.

There were many people on the platform, but everything seemed to move slowly when Maria saw her brother Patrick. She began shouting his name, and as soon as the train came to a full stop, Maria grabbed her luggage and rushed outside.

"There she is!" shouted Patrick, pointing toward Maria as she sprinted toward him for a big hug.

Maria's entire family surrounded her, exchanging hugs for a long time.

"It is so good to see you, sweetheart," said her mother, wiping away her happy tears.

"It's wonderful to have you back home, Maria. We were so happy to hear that you decided to come home," added Maria's father.

"And look at you, sis! Looking great!" exclaimed Maria's youngest brother, Adam, who had fortunately returned home unharmed after the war ended.

Meanwhile, a girl with black hair standing nearby and listening to their conversation caught Maria's attention.

"And, Patrick? Let me guess. This pretty girl is Ana, your lovely wife. Am I right?"

"Yes, she is the girl I was telling you about," responded Patrick, grabbing Ana's hand and bringing her into their circle.

"It is nice to finally meet you, Maria," said Ana.

But before Maria could welcome her sister-in-law into their family with a hug, she felt a hand on her right shoulder and turned to see that it was Delia.

"So, young lady, I hope to see you at the theater soon," said Delia, smiling at Maria.

"I will absolutely think about your offer, Ms. Delia. Until then, it was a pleasure to meet you," responded Maria.

Chapter Fifteen

After the long train ride, Maria enjoyed lounging on the silken cushions of her father's elegant carriage as they rolled along the main street. Since her parents' house was approximately three hours away by carriage, the journey gave them time to reminisce and allowed Maria to get to know her sister-in-law.

It was noon by the time they arrived home, and even though they were exhausted, they stayed awake to talk some more. But after they ate dinner, their fatigue sent them all longingly to bed.

"Thank you for the food, and I wish you goodnight. I'll see you in the morning," said Maria as she walked toward her bedroom.

Maria closed her bedroom door and lay down on her bed. As soon as she closed her eyes, she fell into a deep sleep. Suddenly, a knock at her door woke her. It was dark outside, and it took Maria a few seconds to remember that she was at her parents' house. Unsure if the knock had been real or just a dream, she waited. When she heard another knock, she got out of bed and opened the door.

"Finally, I could wake you up!" said Maria's mother, smiling at her.

"I would like for you to come out and eat something. You should be starving by now," continued her mother.

"Mother, we just finished dinner."

"Oh, sweetheart. That was last night, and you slept all day long. Let's get you some food, and then you can go back to bed."

Maria couldn't believe that she had slept so long, but after she ate some fresh corn porridge with cow's cheese and sour cream and drank a cup of warm cow's milk, she returned to her bedroom to sleep until the next morning, when she woke up to the sound of her brothers talking in the kitchen.

Maria dressed quickly and walked into the kitchen to join their conversation.

"Good morning! Where is Father?" asked Maria when she saw that he was not at the kitchen table.

"It is Sunday. He went to bring some fresh milk from Brown's Farm. He should be back any time," replied Adam.

"And after he returns, we will eat breakfast and then go to church. Would you like to join us?" asked Maria's mother.

"Of course," responded Maria.

During her journey around the country, Maria had the chance to keep some of the dresses that the theater no longer needed. She was excited to share a few of them with her sister-in-law. Ana chose a dark red dress with long sleeves that complemented her hair and skin, which made Patrick smile. Maria selected a black dress with long sleeves adorned with lace and pearls.

"Maria, you look very pretty," said Maria's father as she was putting on her coat.

"Thank you. You look dashing yourself," replied Maria as she admired his black suit and black hat that he was holding in his hand.

Adam looked at himself in the mirror and ran his fingers through his hair. He asked jokingly, "What about me?" as he eagerly awaited compliments.

"All right, handsome! Let's bring the carriage in front of the house for the ladies," said Patrick.

While waiting for the carriage, Katrina's eyes could not hide her sadness, and she looked like she wanted to say something.

"Are you all right, Mother?" asked Maria, noticing something was bothering her.

"Yes, I am all right. But I want to show you something after church," responded Katrina. Then, as she raised her head toward the sky, she asked in an inner voice, "Why, God, could you not allow Maximus and my daughter to grow old together?"

Once they arrived at the church, Adam jumped down from the carriage to help the ladies. They started walking toward the entrance of the church, but as soon as Maria gazed at the crucifix with Jesus nailed to it, she knelt before it, closed her eyes, clasped her hands together, and started to pray.

"Jesus, I am asking for your help. Please show me the right path and give me some answers."

The serene surroundings flooded Maria's brain with memories. She walked down the aisle with Maximus when they were in front of the priest during their wedding ceremony, and "Yes, I do" began looping inside her head.

Suddenly, a breeze parted the leaves of the big tree beside the church, allowing a brief ray of sunlight to shine on Maria's closed eyelids. This unexpected light brought her back to awareness.

Maria touched her face and realized that her eyes were wet with tears. However, more memories bubbled up, pulling her deeper into her past. She remembered the day Maximus was leaving to return to his Army Corps. As she tried to hug him one last time, it seemed that the closer she got, the quicker his figure disappeared into a dense fog.

"Maximus? Where are you?" Maria said out loud.

Immediately, a man's voice called out to Maria from within the thick fog. She stretched her arms out in front of her and walked toward the voice, feeling as if she was just steps away. However, the fog was too dense for her to see clearly, so she continued to reach forward. Then, she caught a glimpse of a hand in the fog. As she reached for it, their hands touched, and her eyes opened.

"Maria, are you all right? Can I help you up?" asked her father, worried that something was wrong.

"Please, everyone, wait for us inside the church while I go for a walk with Maria," stated her mother.

Katrina put her arms around her daughter's shoulders and started walking around the church at a leisurely pace.

"It looks like mom is taking Maria to the cemetery now," said Patrick to his family as he watched them walk away.

Arriving at the entrance of the cemetery, Maria became confused.

"What are we doing here?" she asked.

"I want to show you something," responded her mother as she opened the gate and led the way inside the cemetery.

Walking through certain parts of the cemetery felt like venturing into a jungle. Headstones and tombs had been overtaken by nature, with ivy, roots, and vines spreading across the landscape to create a canopy of natural camouflage. The scene was both eerie and beautiful, as sunlight shone through the gaps in the trees and ivy, casting rippling patterns on the soft grass below.

As Maria and Katrina made their way to the back of the cemetery, Katrina stopped at a polished gray granite headstone. Maria saw Maximus's name engraved in bronze letters, with the dates 1917–1942 beneath it.

"What is this?" asked Maria, startled.

"Sweetheart, we knew that one day you would return home, so your father and I thought that Maximus should have a final resting place—"

But before Katrina could finish her sentence, Maria grabbed the first rock she saw on the ground and frantically started to scrape the death year engraved in the stone as she broke down in tears.

"No! Maximus is not dead! I can still feel he is alive! I can feel it in my heart! He's not dead!"

But once she realized it was impossible to scratch the year off the headstone, Maria stood up and ran all the way home and locked herself in her bedroom. She walked to the window, and as she stared vacantly through the glass, memories from her past came flooding in.

Maria began to see herself with Maximus on the coldest days when they pulled each other on a sled on their way to school. She remembered the night when Maximus saved her from two drunk men and the moment when Maximus waited for her in the park to ask her to marry him. Suddenly, a peculiar sound from outside brought Maria back to reality. She opened her eyes, and as she looked outside through the window, Maria nearly jumped out of her skin when she saw in the reflection that Maximus was reaching toward her. Slowly, she turned around, and as soon she saw Maximus, time seemed to stop.

They both stood there, staring at each other, but when Maria went to hug him, her body went straight through him. She quickly turned around to try flinging her arms back around him, but her arms passed through his body once again as his image began to vanish.

Maria dropped to her knees with her hands on her face and began to plead with Maximus to not leave her again. Her body started rocking back and forth involuntarily.

"Oh, my poor baby," cooed her mother as she held Maria and rocked her gently.

"I truly apologize for the headstone we made for Maximus, and I am sorry if that hurt you," continued

Katrina as she delicately ran her hand through Maria's hair.

Maria knew her parents did not intend to hurt her feelings, but she was not ready to admit that her husband would be gone forever.

"Mother, I understand that what you and Father have done for me was for my own good, but lately, I've been dreaming a lot about Maximus, and I refuse to believe that he's dead. Something in my heart tells me that he is still alive, and I believe that something will bring us back together," replied Maria confidently.

Chapter Sixteen

Even though Maria was back home and surrounded by loved ones, she still felt lonely. Her father and Patrick were away from home from morning until night, as they had to commute every day to the city for their job, working as butchers at the Slaughter Warehouse. Adam was working the second shift at a leather factory in the neighboring village, and Katrina was not only taking care of her house, but she was also helping Ana, who was pregnant, around her house.

Maria felt the need to keep herself busy as well. On the first Monday of April, as winter allowed spring to reveal its warmer days, she decided to take into consideration Ms. Delia's invitation and pay her a visit at the theater, hoping that her job offer was still good.

The commute to the city from Maria's house needed to happen by bus, and there were only three buses scheduled a day.

For those starting their first shift at 8:00 a.m., the first bus from the village was scheduled to depart at

5:30 a.m., arriving in the city at 7:30 a.m. The second bus was scheduled to leave at 9:00 a.m., and the third bus was set to depart at 11:30 a.m., arriving in the city by 1:30 p.m. for the second shift that began at 2:00 p.m. For the return trip, the buses were scheduled at 2:30 p.m., 5:00 p.m., and the last one at 10:30 p.m.

Maria took the nine o'clock bus and arrived at the city's main station at 11:00 a.m. From there, it took her another ten minutes to walk to the Romanian National Theater. Before climbing the stairs at the theater's entrance, she paused to admire the building's elegance. The facade featured three arched portals and two shorter towers, each topped with a statue of a person riding a chariot drawn by lions. Each statue symbolically held a palm branch.

"Hello, Maria. Are you wondering who those two statues represent?" someone asked unexpectedly.

Maria turned her head curiously to see who recognized her, and she was pleasantly surprised to see Ms. Delia, who continued to explain about the statues as she pointed at them.

"The National Theater was officially opened on September 18, 1919, simultaneously with the Romanian Opera, both sharing the same building. So the two statues are muses who represent theater and opera. Terpsichore, the statue on the left, is the muse of music and dance, and Thalia is the muse of comedy and theater. But let's go inside, and I will give you a tour of the theater. Then we can have a cup of tea together, although I really hope that you are here because of the offer I made on the train," continued Ms. Delia.

After a pleasant conversation and a cup of tea, Maria gladly accepted Ms. Delia's offer to return to work at the theater as a costume designer and seamstress. Even though her commute made her days much longer—taking the 11:30 a.m. bus and arriving home around midnight—Maria didn't mind. The work kept her mind occupied and helped distract her from thoughts of Maximus.

As winter approached and the days grew shorter, Maria decided to move to the city. She secured a small, affordable studio right outside downtown, reducing her commute from four hours by bus to a fifteen-minute walk. However, Maria still visited her family whenever she could, especially since she had recently become an aunt. Ana had given birth to a baby girl, whom she and Patrick named Felicia.

Everything seemed to be working out for Maria. Working at the theater kept her mind occupied, and she even brought home costumes to tailor when she needed something to do. However, as weeks turned into months and months into years, Maria's pattern of daily life started to feel monotonous and exhausting. Her longing for her husband resurfaced, and she felt drained by returning to an empty home every night. Although her studio was filled with dresses and rolls of fabric waiting to be transformed into beautiful creations, Maria craved companionship. However, she wasn't looking for the company of another man.

Maria decided to purchase a three-bedroom apartment in the city with the money she saved over the years. She invited her brother Patrick and his family, who were expecting another child, to move in with her, as Patrick still had to commute every day to work in the city by bus.

The prospect of an easier life was too good for Patrick and his family to pass up. With only a few weeks left before Patrick's wife was due to give birth, they eagerly moved into Maria's new apartment.

The move brought positive changes for everyone. Maria quickly became an important part of her brother's family, and the birth of her nephew brought her joy and a renewed sense of purpose. Patrick and Ana even let Maria choose a name for their son, and she proudly chose the name Octavian.

Maria loved taking care of Octavian whenever she had the chance, but she was needed the most for raising Octavian after Ana's maternity leave ended and she had to return to work. However, since Maria had already offered her apartment to Patrick's family as their new home in the city, Patrick and Ana didn't want to take advantage of Maria's kindness when she offered to care for their son during the day. So they decided to enroll him in the same childcare where their daughter spent her days happily.

Nevertheless, on Octavian's first day at childcare, he started crying and asked his aunt to go back home with him. Maria felt heartbroken seeing the sadness in Octavian's eyes when she left him there, but she continued to drop him off at childcare for the rest of the week, trying to respect Patrick and Ana's wishes. However, after sharing their feelings with Patrick and Ana, they kindly accepted Maria's offer to care for Octavian while they were at work. From that moment on, Maria and Octavian spent their days together, forming a close bond and enjoying various experiences.

Some days, Maria and Octavian would walk in the park, while on others, they would explore the city and learn about its history. They might have a picnic by the forest near their apartment or simply sit by the river near their church, enjoying nature.

Every Sunday, they had a routine—Maria would take Octavian to church in the morning, followed by a family lunch at home. Then, they would visit Maria's favorite place, the theater, where Octavian would be placed in the balcony seats on the first level, making him feel like a part of the play. The theater soon became one of Octavian's favorite places, too.

As Octavian turned six years old, the bond between him and Maria grew stronger and deeper. Maria's kindness and constant companionship made her more than just an aunt; she became like a second mother to Octavian, providing comfort in any circumstance. Consequently, it became difficult for Octavian to leave his aunt during summer vacation when he and his sister Felicia had to visit their grandparents in the village for two months at a time.

The reason Patrick and Ana sent their children to their grandparents was to give them a taste of farm life, just like they had experienced growing up. They enjoyed activities such as chasing chickens through the yard, which was a lot of fun, and the messy job of feeding pigs. Learning how to brush and pet horses and sheep was very exciting as well. Additionally, the children found climbing trees and enjoying the fruit at the end of an adventurous climb to be rewarding.

However, this year was different as Octavian would start first grade soon after returning home from the farm. He wanted to spend more time with his aunt, so he tried to convince his parents to let him stay at home instead of going to the farm. Despite his efforts, Octavian still found himself at the farm, counting down the days until he could return to his aunt.

Usually, Patrick and Ana would arrive first thing in the morning, around 7:00 a.m. on Sunday, to pick up the children. This would give them plenty of time to get back to the city before church mass began. However, on that particular day, it was already 8:45 a.m., and Octavian was still impatiently waiting on the bench in front of his grandparents' house for his parents to arrive.

Half an hour later, his parents still had not arrived. As time passed, Octavian became more and more impatient. Unfortunately, he had no choice but to continue waiting restlessly on the bench, looking down the road in hopes of seeing his parents' car appear.

Time continued to pass, and Octavian's parents were still not in sight. Octavian had not taken his eyes off of the road. Suddenly, he shouted happily, "I see them!

They're finally here!" and began to run toward the house to grab his backpack.

However, by the time Octavian's parents said goodbye to his grandparents and got into the car, it was already 10:30 a.m. They realized it would be impossible to make it back home before noon, so Octavian would likely miss the entire mass. Regardless, Patrick decided to drive directly to the church to see if they could find Maria, even though the service would be over. After all, a promise was still a promise.

Once they arrived at the church, people were already leaving. Since Maria was usually one of the last to exit, Octavian decided to hide right outside the open doors in order to surprise her.

Octavian eagerly waited behind the door to catch a glimpse of his aunt. However, since she had not appeared yet, he risked ruining the surprise by taking another peek inside the church to see if he could locate her. Suddenly, he felt a hand on his shoulder.

This startled him, but when he turned around, he saw that it was Mrs. Joanna, one of Maria's good friends.

"Octavian? Is that you? I haven't seen you in a while. What are you doing here all by yourself?" she asked.

"Hello, Mrs. Joanna. I am waiting for my aunt. I am trying to surprise her. Have you seen her?" he asked curiously.

Yes, I saw her. But she left about twenty minutes ago before mass was over. She didn't look well, and I am worried about her. When I asked her if she was all right, she told me that she was fine and that she was going to the river.

As soon as Octavian heard Mrs. Joanna say her aunt went to the river, he knew exactly where she would be, and he started running as fast as his legs could carry him toward the river.

During the mass, Maria started to feel dizzy and nauseous, and her vision became blurry. She didn't know what was happening to her or how to react, so she decided to go outside for some fresh air and take a nice walk along the Little Somes River.

That place was one of her favorite places because it always made her feel peaceful with its calm surroundings. The sound of the wind and the water splashing over the rocks, which blended together with music made by tiny musicians dressed in colorful feathers, reminded her of the soothing symphony.

But when Maria believed she was feeling better, she suddenly got struck with a severe headache and fell to the ground, leaving her to lie there alone, staring at the blue sky, frozen in fear.

Then she heard a voice . . .

"Aunt Maria! Aunt Maria!"

It was Octavian's voice, shouting for her as he tried to find her, yet he couldn't see that his aunt was lying flat on the grass.

Maria tried to answer, but she couldn't, and then she became unconscious.

It lasted about two minutes, and the second her eyes opened, Octavian was next to her, crying out for help from Patrick, who was not too far behind him.

Maria's face had drooped on the left side, and it seemed like she had difficulties moving, mostly her left arm and her left leg.

"Father, what's happening with Aunt Maria?" asked Octavian with concern as he watched his aunt motionless on the ground.

"Son! Quickly, run back to the church and tell the priest to call for an ambulance. And then wait for the ambulance. When they arrive, show them how to get here."

Octavian raced back to the church without stopping or looking back while Patrick stayed by Maria's side.

"What happened to you, Maria?" he asked.

Maria understood her brother, but she could not speak. Could it be appendicitis? Heart attack? Stroke? The possibilities whirled around in Patrick's head, and waiting for the ambulance was the longest twenty minutes of his life.

Two paramedics got out of the vehicle as soon as it stopped. One carried a first aid kit, while the other opened the back doors and pulled out a stretcher. Right behind them, Octavian hurriedly exited from the front passenger side and ran straight to his aunt. Her eyes were open, and she was breathing normally, but unfortunately, she remained motionless. After the paramedics examined Maria carefully, they gently put her on the stretcher to take her to the hospital.

"It's thanks to your swift action that your aunt might be all right. If she had been left here any longer, who knows what might have happened," said one of the paramedics to Octavian.

"May I ride in the back of the ambulance with my aunt?" asked Octavian as he watched them secure the stretcher inside the ambulance. "I just want to hold my aunt's hand."

The paramedic felt sympathy for Octavian and said it would be all right if they had his father's permission.

"Go ahead, son. We'll see you at the hospital," responded Patrick.

Octavian jumped into the back of the ambulance and sat on a small bench attached to the wall next to his aunt. He held her hand as the ambulance raced through the city streets.

Once they reached the ER, a doctor and nurses rolled Maria into one of the main treatment rooms, where they started the acute heart failure protocol.

Everyone knew what to do, but when they didn't find anything wrong with Maria's heart, the doctor assumed she had experienced a ruptured aneurysm. Unfortunately, there wasn't anything he could do, as there were no specialists in the city, and only time would reveal her fate.

By the time Patrick reached the hospital room, Maria was lying in the bed with her eyes shut. The doctor was still standing beside her while Octavian held her hand. Although Maria wasn't moving, Patrick could see her chest slowly moving up and down, and he knew she wasn't dead.

"Son, are you all right?" asked Patrick with tears in his eyes.

"Yes," he uttered.

"You must be Maria's brother. Your son was just telling me how he found his aunt and that you should be on your way here," stated the doctor.

"I prayed all the way here that my sister would be all right. How is she, Doctor?" asked Patrick with high hopes to hear only good news about his sister.

"I believe your sister had a ruptured aneurysm. Fortunately, it didn't kill her, but it still led to oxygen deprivation in part of her brain, leaving her incapable of moving the left side of her body as well as hindering her ability to communicate. At this point, we can only hope for the best," responded the doctor.

Maria was supposed to be at the theater that evening to help with a play scheduled to start at 7:00 p.m. No one at the theater knew what had happened to her. However, Maria had never missed a day of work or been late in all her time there, so her absence raised concern, especially for Ms. Delia. Over the ten years that Maria worked at the theater for Ms. Delia, she had become like the daughter Ms. Delia had always wanted.

Ms. Delia was once married like Maria, but sadly, she became a war widow because of World War I, and she never got married again. So it was easy to connect with Maria because she understood what Maria was going through.

When the play ended and Maria was still missing, Ms. Delia went straight to Maria's apartment. There,

Ana explained what had happened and described Maria's condition. Concerned, Ms. Delia rushed to the hospital. After seeing Maria's condition with her own eyes, she immediately formulated a plan to help her.

"Tonight, I will call my dear friend Dr. Klaus Friedrich, who is in charge of one of the best clinics in Munich, Germany. Tomorrow, I will have everything organized and prepared for Maria to get there safely. I have known Dr. Klaus for more than ten years now, and I know he would provide the best rehab for Maria. What do you think, Patrick?" asked Ms. Delia, hoping he would give her permission.

"Thank you, Ms. Delia, and I appreciate you trying to help my sister. Everything sounds good as long as I can go with her because I don't want my sister to be alone. Plus, I can speak some German, and that would make it easier for everyone," responded Patrick.

"And I would like to go as well," said Octavian.

That night, Ms. Delia took care of everything. She organized the transportation from the hospital to the train station, where Maria, Patrick, and Octavian had a private compartment reserved for them the next morning on a train that would take them to Budapest. From there, she scheduled another train to go directly to the main station in Munich, where Dr. Klaus said he would personally wait for them.

Chapter Seventeen

Ms. Delia's plan ran smoothly, and Maria, Patrick, and Octavian arrived in Munich safely. Dr. Klaus, along with a paramedic from his clinic, were waiting with a stretcher for Maria on the arrival platform.

"Okay, son. Stay with your aunt while I find Dr. Klaus," said Patrick as the train came to a stop.

Once Patrick stepped off the train, he immediately saw the doctor because someone next to him was wearing a white medical gown and holding a sign that read "Maria."

"Hello, Dr. Klaus. I am Patrick, Maria's brother. First of all, I want to thank you for being available to help my sister," said Patrick in German, which surprised Dr. Klaus.

"Good to meet you, Patrick. I am surprised at how well you can speak German. Let's go and take your sister from the train, and maybe later you can tell me when you learned German," said Dr. Klaus.

Shortly after Maria was secured onto the stretcher, she was taken to the ambulance that Dr. Klaus had waiting for them.

"Patrick, the paramedic will take care of Maria from here. You and your son are welcome to come with me in my car. We are going to the clinic, and once I have Maria set up in her room, I will take you to the hotel, where I reserved a room for you and your son."

The ride to the clinic was only thirty minutes away from the train station. Once Maria was placed into a private room, Patrick was relieved to find that the hotel where he and his son were staying was right across the street from the clinic.

"This is your room, and now, I will let you get a good night's sleep. You should be exhausted," said Dr. Klaus as he finished showing Patrick and Octavian their room.

"I cannot express how grateful I am that you can help my sister," responded Patrick as he shook Dr. Klaus's hand.

"You know, when I received a phone call from Delia, I was delighted to hear her voice again. And after she told me your sister's story, I was proud that Delia thought of me to help your sister. Tomorrow, Dr. Muller, one of my best doctors, will examine Maria, and he should be in her room by eight o'clock to start the recovery process. So I will most likely see you sometime tomorrow. Until then, get some rest," said Dr. Klaus as he opened the door to leave.

The night passed like a blink of an eye, and since the window from their room was left uncovered, the sun started to slowly pierce through the window at the crack of dawn, waking Patrick and Octavian.

Patrick's eyes opened wide, and as he looked at the time, he saw that Octavian was awake as well.

"Good morning, Father. What time is it?" asked Octavian as he squinted from the sun.

"Good morning. It is ten minutes to seven. How did you sleep?"

"I slept pretty well. I feel rested and ready to see Aunt Maria."

"Then let's go keep her company before Dr. Muller gets there," responded Patrick.

When they entered Maria's room, Maria was wide awake.

"Good morning, sister. Good morning, Auntie," said Patrick to Octavian as they walked over to give her a kiss on her cheek.

Maria's eyes widened as she held out her open hand, waiting for Octavian to take it. Then, she made an incomprehensible sound, perhaps trying to say, "Good morning!" in response.

"What did you say, Aunt Maria?" asked Octavian, looking into her eyes.

Sadly, they struggled to understand what Maria was trying to communicate. Seeing Octavian's confusion only added to her frustration.

"Please don't get mad, Auntie. Everything will be all right. The doctor will make you better."

"And we are not going anywhere until you get better," continued Patrick as he grabbed both of their hands.

Suddenly, there were three knocks at the door, and then the door slowly began to open. It was Dr. Klaus, accompanied by Dr. Muller.

"Good morning. This is Dr. Muller, and he is one of our best," said Dr. Klaus as they both approached Maria's bed.

"Good morning. It is good to meet you, and it is such a relief that my sister will be in such good hands," responded Patrick in German as he shook Dr. Muller's hand.

"Dr. Klaus already told me that you speak some German, but I am really impressed with your accent."

"Thank you," said Patrick.

"Once we have a complete report and determine the best treatment for your sister, your German will come in handy for translating. But first, let me introduce myself to your sister," continued Dr. Muller.

Since Octavian was not included in the conversation, he stepped to the side of the room, sat down in a chair, and listened quietly.

"Hello, Maria. I'm Dr. Muller. It's a pleasure to meet you. You're in the right place, and we'll take good care of you," said Dr. Muller, holding Maria's left hand gently.

"Patrick, could you please tell your sister that I'd like to listen to her heart?" he added as he grabbed his stethoscope.

Dr. Muller carefully opened Maria's shirt just enough to place his stethoscope on her chest. As he listened to her heartbeat, his eyes widened, and he stared at her suspiciously. His expression grew increasingly puzzled as he continued to examine her.

"I am surprised to see dog tags around your sister's neck. It is unusual for a lady to wear," said Dr. Muller as he looked down at his notebook. He began writing while alternately looking at the notebook and Maria's dog tags.

But before Dr. Muller could get any details from Patrick about the dog tags, one of the nurses rushed into the room and said that the doctor was urgently needed on the second floor.

"It is very hard to find a good doctor like Dr. Muller. He is experienced when it comes to emergencies. He was a German lieutenant, as well as a physician during World War II," said Dr. Klaus as Dr. Muller left the room in a hurry with the nurse. "But, he will be back shortly to continue Maria's examination. Until then, I am going to see what the emergency is upstairs."

In the meantime, Octavian couldn't take his eyes off the notebook that Dr. Muller left behind.

"Why do you think Dr. Muller was so interested in Aunt Maria's dog tags?" Octavian asked his father.

"Why are you asking? Did you understand Dr. Muller asking me about the dog tags?"

"No! But, I saw him writing down information about the dog tags in his notebook."

"Dr. Muller might have written down something related to Maria, and now that Dr. Klaus told me that Dr. Muller was an SS lieutenant, as well as a physician during World War II, he was probably just curious about the dog tags. Plus, since he said it is unusual to see dog tags around a woman's neck, maybe he just wanted to know why she was wearing them."

"But, I saw him writing down Maximus's name and . . . You know what? Let me show you!" Octavian stood up from his chair and grabbed Dr. Muller's notebook.

"Son! Put it down. I don't think Dr. Muller would appreciate you looking through his notebook."

"But, Dad! Look! I told you. He wrote down information from Aunt Maria's dog tags," exclaimed Octavian as he showed his dad the notebook.

Patrick read, "Maximus D. Army Corps Border Division," written down on one of the pages, and that surprised him as well.

"It is interesting. Why would he write that down?" Patrick asked himself out loud.

Suddenly, there was a knock at the door, so Octavian quickly put down the notebook on the small table next to Maria's bed. By the time the door opened, he was already sitting down on the bed by his aunt's feet.

Dr. Muller came back down with one of the male nurses who was working there.

"All right. Now that everything is under control upstairs, I should be able to focus on you, Maria," said Dr. Muller. "Oh, I did not realize I left my notebook here," he continued as if forgetting it wasn't a big deal.

He clearly remembered leaving his notebook on Maria's bed, but now that it was on her bedside table, he subtly observed Patrick and Octavian's reactions as he picked it up.

"Yes, you left it on the bed when you left in a hurry," Patrick replied smoothly. "My son moved it to the table so he could sit next to his aunt."

Maria overheard the conversation between Patrick and Octavian, which made her feel uneasy about Dr. Muller.

"After I develop an individualized plan for Maria, I will need you to translate it to her so she will learn about her recovery process. But before that, let's take the dog tags off of her neck since she will be moved around a lot," said Dr. Muller.

But as soon as Dr. Muller tried to take them, Maria clutched them tightly with her right hand and wouldn't let go.

"Is there anything I need to know?" asked Dr. Muller as he witnessed Maria's reaction.

"The dog tags around my sister's neck are the only things that were found after her husband disappeared during World War II. Since that's all she has left of him, she has never taken them off after she received them from the Romanian army. So I know my sister would prefer to keep them on her neck throughout her recovery process if possible."

"That shouldn't be a problem. However, sometimes, I will need to take them off for her safety. But you can tell your sister that she will get them back," replied Dr. Muller. "Now, the nurse will need to take your sister down the hallway for some tests, which should take about two hours. After that, once she has her medication with some food, she will probably want to sleep for a couple of hours.

Also, please tell your sister that throughout the day, we'll need to move her around to different rooms, depending on the treatment, but she will always be brought back to this room by the end of the day. If you'd like, you can come back later to check on her," Dr. Muller continued.

"I would like that. But before we leave, I'd like to ask for a recommendation on where we can eat that is close," asked Patrick.

"Three blocks away, there is a place that serves breakfast and is within walking distance from here. If you're looking for other restaurants, you'll need to catch a bus or take a cab downtown," recommended Dr. Muller.

"For now, we'll eat at the restaurant that is only three blocks away," responded Patrick. After he thanked the doctor, he walked over to Maria's bed to translate what the doctor told him.

"Don't worry, Auntie. By the time you're wide awake in your room, Father and I will be here too, I promise!" Octavian said before leaving with his father. He gave her a kiss on the cheek before he left.

Later that afternoon, when Maria woke up from a long, deep rest, she felt instant joy, and her eyes sparkled upon seeing Patrick and Octavian sitting by her bed. She tried to speak but could only make sounds that Patrick and Octavian could barely understand.

"Maria! It's all right. We are here, and we'll go through this together," said Patrick as he took Maria's hand to comfort her because she seemed troubled.

Maria nodded yes to let Patrick know she understood him, but her eyes began to fill with tears.

"Let's have faith, sister. Only faith could have brought us all the way here," continued Patrick.

When Octavian saw his aunt begin to cry, he gently took her hand and said to her, "You'll be okay, Auntie. You'll be okay."

Maria slowly pulled Octavian toward her for a hug, and she gave him a smile.

"Would you like to have some water?" asked Patrick as he noticed Maria's lips looked chapped.

With a nod of her head telling him yes, Patrick walked toward the table to bring her a cup of water, but the water pitcher was completely empty.

"I'll be right back. I am going to the cafeteria to get some water," he said.

Dr. Muller's office was on the way to the cafeteria, so Patrick thought he would stop by to ask about Maria's first treatment. However, as he approached the office, he heard a muffled conversation that sounded like a disagreement. Not wanting to interrupt, he decided to continue walking toward the cafeteria instead.

As he turned the corner, he heard the office door open. Deciding to see if Dr. Muller was in, he started to head back. But as he turned around, he realized that the conversation had moved into the hallway. Patrick recognized the other voice—it was the male nurse who had helped his sister earlier.

"Listen! Tonight, you will bring me her dog tags, and tomorrow, we'll transport her to my house by ambulance," Dr. Muller told the nurse.

Once Patrick heard that they were talking about his sister, he took a few steps closer to the office and stood there, out of sight, secretly listening to their conversation.

"I will say it again, Dr. Muller. I believe that it's too soon and it's too risky. Let's wait for a few more days."

"We have to do it now because Dr. Klaus leaves this afternoon, and he will be out of the city for two days. Nobody will find out about it, and that's it. So I'm expecting you to do what you are told," continued Dr. Muller, trying his best not to raise his voice as he looked left and right, checking to see if anybody was around.

Patrick was utterly confused by what he had just overheard Dr. Muller saying, and he didn't feel comfortable talking to him at that moment. So he quietly turned around and headed to the cafeteria to get some water. However, he couldn't stop thinking about why Dr. Muller wanted the nurse to take Maria's dog tags tonight when she was not scheduled for any treatments and why he planned to take her to his house.

Patrick and Octavian stayed with Maria at the clinic for the rest of the day. After Maria had her dinner and medicine and fell asleep, Patrick decided it was time for them to go to the motel and get some rest as well.

"Your aunt seems peaceful. Let's go back to the motel," said Patrick to his son, who was sitting on the chair next to Maria's head.

"May I stay a bit longer? I am not that tired," asked Octavian.

"All right, but not for too long. It's going to get dark soon, so I need you to be at the motel before that," responded Patrick.

But as soon as Patrick walked out of the room, Octavian stood up from the chair and left the room as well.

"What happened, son? Have you already changed your mind?" asked Patrick after he turned around since he could hear footsteps behind him, and he saw Octavian.

"No, I just have to go to the restroom."

"Then, I'll see you at the hotel. But remember, be back at the motel before dark," Patrick said as they arrived at the washroom, located at the end of the hallway across from the stairs leading to the main exit of the clinic.

"Yes, Father," Octavian replied.

After descending the stairs, Patrick exited the building. The male nurse who was working with Dr. Muller noticed him leave and realized the boy was not with him. Assuming the boy might have left the clinic before his father or that he had not seen him, the nurse immediately headed toward Maria's room.

Just as the nurse was about to enter Maria's room, Octavian emerged from the bathroom and saw him opening the door. Quietly, Octavian tiptoed behind the nurse and was surprised to see him trying carefully to remove the dog tags from Maria without waking her.

Octavian wanted to ask the nurse why he was doing this, but since he did not speak German, he decided to silently observe to see if the nurse would succeed. When the nurse finally managed to take the dog tags without waking Maria, Octavian quickly and quietly slipped away. He hurried back to the motel room, where his father had just lain down to relax.

"Father, I just saw the nurse take the dog tags from Aunt Maria's neck while she was asleep!" exclaimed Octavian the second he entered the door.

"Perhaps the nurse had to move her into another room, and he needed to take them off for her safety," said Patrick.

"But she was sleeping! Shouldn't he have woken her up first before removing the dog tags if he was going to move her somewhere?" asked Octavian.

"You know what, let's just go check on her!" Patrick said as he stood up from the bed. He tried to keep his anger in check, especially remembering the conversation he had overheard in the hallway between Dr. Muller and the nurse a few hours ago.

Once they arrived at Maria's room, Patrick slowly opened the door so he could take a peek inside, and they saw Maria, who was by herself, sleeping peacefully.

"Let's try not to wake her up," whispered Patrick as they quietly walked inside the room.

"Look, Dad," whispered Octavian as he pointed at his aunt's neck.

"Why would the nurse do that?" Patrick asked himself once he realized that his sister's dog tags were missing from around her neck.

Patrick couldn't find any reasonable explanation why Dr. Muller would ask the nurse to take Maria's dog tags, so he decided to go and find Dr. Muller or the nurse to ask. But he couldn't find them anywhere. Dr. Muller was already at his house, and Patrick and Octavian just missed the nurse who left the clinic before they walked down into the lobby.

"We'll have to find out what's going on tomorrow. But for now, let's let your aunt sleep and go back to our room and rest as well," said Patrick to his son, bothered that he couldn't get an explanation.

It was natural for Patrick to be upset about what happened to his sister and to seek answers. Being far from home and surrounded by unfamiliar people made it even harder to trust them. Despite this, as he lay in bed, unable to sleep, Patrick had to convince himself to trust those who were supposed to help Maria.

As Patrick repeated to himself that there must be a good explanation for what happened to his sister's dog tags, he finally began to drift off to sleep. By morning, he awoke and told Octavian to get up so they could check on Maria before she discovered her dog tags were missing. He didn't want to leave his sister alone, upset and intimidated by the situation, especially since she couldn't speak German. They were ready in less than ten minutes and soon arrived at Maria's room.

Luckily, Maria was still asleep, so Patrick and Octavian took seats and waited patiently for her to wake. When the door opened slowly, as if someone was trying to peek inside without being noticed, they saw Dr. Muller. Realizing Maria was not alone, he quickly withdrew.

"Dr. Muller," Patrick said loudly enough to make sure he would get the doctor's attention.

Dr. Muller acted as though he couldn't hear and continued walking down the hallway toward his office.

"Dr. Muller!" Patrick called out again, stepping out of the room and closing the door behind him as he followed Dr. Muller down the hall.

Unable to ignore Patrick any longer, Dr. Muller finally stopped and turned to address him.

"Good morning, Patrick. You're here earlier than I expected. I meant earlier than yesterday," the doctor corrected himself.

Patrick noticed that the doctor was still dressed in a suit and carrying a briefcase, indicating that he had just arrived at the clinic much earlier than he had previously mentioned.

"Good morning, Dr. Muller," responded Patrick.

"Is everything all right? It seemed like you wanted to visit my sister earlier, but you changed your mind as soon as you saw me and my son sitting next to her," asked Patrick curiously.

"I just wanted to check on your sister, and once I saw you and your son, I didn't want to disturb you. But I will go back later to check on her," responded Dr. Muller abruptly.

"Oh! One more question, Dr. Muller. This morning, I noticed that my sister's dog tags are missing. Do you have any idea where they could be? I would like to give them back to her as soon as she wakes."

"I just got here. But let me check with the nurse. Maybe he knows where they are," answered Dr. Muller with an extremely convincing honest look on his face.

But as the doctor switched his briefcase from his right hand to his left and turned to walk toward his office, Patrick noticed a chain with red and yellow colors hanging out of his right pocket. It looked very much like Maria's.

Those are definitely Maria's dog tags, Patrick said to himself, uncertain why the doctor lied about them.

Patrick remembered that when Maria received Maximus's dog tags from the Romanian army, she had painted a small portion of the chain with yellow and red to symbolize hope and strength. Recognizing the chain in Dr. Muller's pocket, he decided to follow him to his office to uncover the truth. Just as he was preparing to confront the doctor, the office door suddenly opened.

"Oh!" the doctor said nervously. "Look, I found Maria's dog tags on my desk, and I wanted to bring them to you right away. Perhaps the nurse left them on my desk," continued the doctor as he showed Patrick the dog tags.

Patrick took the dog tags from the doctor's hand, and after a quick glance at the doctor's coat pocket, it only proved the doctor lied again.

"Thank you. I am glad they're not lost. I will take them to my sister right away," said Patrick without asking him anything else since the doctor would probably come up with another lie.

Chapter Eighteen

Patrick returned to Maria's room, hoping that Dr. Muller's intentions were good. After all, he did return the dog tags. However, given the doctor's previous lies and his plan to take Maria from the clinic that evening by ambulance, Patrick decided he needed a plan to keep his sister safe.

So when he and his son left the clinic around 8:30 p.m., they got into a taxi and asked the driver to wait at the corner of the clinic, the best spot to observe if Maria would be taken out.

Two hours passed at a snail's pace as they waited in the car. Since the taxi driver had agreed to an hourly rental fee, whether driving or not, he seemed the most patient of the three.

Another hour passed, and still nothing.

"We'll probably wait here until midnight, and if nothing happens by then, perhaps—"

"Dad, look! The ambulance is moving!" interrupted Octavian.

"Okay, wait here!" said Patrick to his son as he got out of the taxi so he could take a closer look and see if the ambulance was taking Maria.

The driver didn't care about what was going on, but when Patrick got back into the cab and instructed him to follow the ambulance, the driver was reluctant to do so.

"I will pay you more money," said Patrick to the taxi driver as he watched the ambulance pull out from the clinic's parking lot.

"It's not about the money! I just don't want to follow an ambulance with flashing lights," the taxi driver replied, pointing at the ambulance. As the ambulance pulled out onto the street, the lights unexpectedly turned off.

"Look! Now the lights are off!" shouted Patrick. "Now, can you start following the ambulance?" pleaded Patrick.

The taxi driver agreed to follow the ambulance as long as the flashing lights were turned off. At Patrick's request, the driver maintained a safe distance to avoid detection. Half an hour later, while they were still pursuing the ambulance on the main road outside the city, the ambulance abruptly turned right onto a narrow private road that led deeper into the forest.

"Keep driving straight and pull over once we pass the road where the ambulance turned," said Patrick to the driver.

Once the taxi stopped, Patrick considered walking to the end of the road. However, because it was pitch dark and he was unfamiliar with the forest, he did not feel comfortable bringing his son along.

"Dad, why did we stop following them?" Octavian asked, interrupting his father's thoughts.

"If we had turned right as well, it would have been too obvious that we were following them. And now I don't know what else we should do. Let me think," responded Patrick.

Meanwhile, the driver noticed Patrick's strange behavior and anxious energy, which made him uncomfortable. "So what now?" the taxi driver asked Patrick. "Nothing makes sense to me. I don't understand what you are trying to do, but I will not continue to wait here. I don't care if you agree or not. I am leaving right now!" continued the taxi driver as he turned on the engine.

"Wait just a second! I will try my best to explain to you the reason why we followed the ambulance, but please don't leave yet."

Once the driver understood why they were following the ambulance, his patience increased, and he became curious enough to listen to the rest of Patrick's explanation.

"You know, that certainly seems suspicious. And, if you want to go and see what's going on with your sister, your son will be safe with me," said the taxi driver, realizing the circumstances.

Just as Patrick opened the door, two headlights appeared through the trees, coming down the same road the ambulance had taken.

"Please turn off your headlights!" Patrick shouted. "I can't tell if it's the ambulance, but someone's coming this way." He quickly closed the door and began to stare through the rear window.

"Yes, it is the ambulance, and they are heading back to the city," continued Patrick.

"What do you want me to do?" asked the driver, seeming a bit more intrigued to find out additional bits and pieces about what was going on.

The ambulance was quickly vanishing into the darkness, so Patrick needed to make a decision quickly. Either follow the ambulance without knowing if his sister was inside or go check to see if she was in the area where she was taken.

"I really need to see why the doctor needed to bring my sister all the way here secretly!" said Patrick to the taxi driver with some rage in his voice.

Then, Patrick took a deep breath to steady himself, told Octavian to wait in the car, opened the door, and walked toward the narrow road that led deeper into the woods.

The dense trees almost blocked out the moonlight, making the path difficult to navigate. As he ventured further, he spotted some lights ahead, indicating the end of the road. Once he arrived at a camouflaged wooden cabin, he noticed a car parked nearby.

He did not see anybody outside, so he approached the cabin's only window and quietly looked inside. Patrick was surprised that he didn't see anybody, but that only made him feel uneasy since he saw a car and the lights were on.

Somebody has to be around, he thought to himself.

Patrick decided to hide next to the cabin until he felt safe enough to continue investigating. As he turned to find a hiding spot, he saw movement inside the cabin. To his surprise, a wall started to open, revealing Dr. Muller emerging from what appeared to be a secret room.

Patrick stayed hidden while peering through the window. He saw Dr. Muller grab a syringe and a small clear bottle from a drawer in the kitchen. After he pulled the liquid into the syringe and squirted a little bit out, he walked back through the secret door.

Noticing that there were no other people outside, Patrick circled the cabin, checking for any openings that might give him access to the secret room. However, the cabin had only one door and one window. To find out if the syringe was meant for Maria, Patrick would need to enter through the front door, risking being caught. But he was determined to help his sister and knew she would do the same for him.

After one last look through the window, Patrick walked to the front door and slowly opened it. As he stepped inside, the old wooden floor creaked loudly with each step, creating a noise like an alarm.

Patrick's intention was to open the secret door and see if Maria was there. But he suddenly heard footsteps approaching the door. With nowhere to hide, he rushed outside as quickly and quietly as he could to hide. Realizing he had left the door open, he cautiously went back to close it, trying not to leave any sign of his presence. Just then, he heard someone coming his way in the shadows of the forest. He quickly hid around the corner to see who might appear.

To Patrick's surprise, it was Octavian and the taxi driver. The driver, speaking in German, repeatedly asked Octavian to wait for him. He wasn't loud, but the still and quiet forest seemed to amplify the sound of his voice, which carried through the open cabin door that Dr. Muller had not yet noticed.

Dr. Muller wasn't expecting anyone, so when he heard a voice from outside, he pulled a pistol out of the holster hidden underneath his shirt. Ready to shoot, he walked out of the cabin to see who was outside.

"Don't move, or I'll shoot!" yelled Dr. Muller as soon as he saw two dark silhouettes approaching the cabin.

Octavian and the taxi driver stopped moving instantly when they noticed the pistol aimed straight at them.

"Now, slowly walk toward me with your hands up! Let's see who the fuck you are and why you are on my property!" continued Dr. Muller.

The moment Dr. Muller could see their faces, he easily recognized Octavian, but he didn't recognize the man next to him. This made the doctor uneasy and paranoid, wondering how much they knew about what was going on in the cabin.

"Who the fuck are you, and where's Patrick? Where's the boy's father? And how did you know about this place?" asked the doctor, enraged as he pointed the pistol at the man he didn't recognize.

"Answer me, or I will shoot you right now!" continued the doctor, yelling at the driver.

After the doctor's reaction, Patrick realized that the doctor definitely seemed to be hiding something in the cabin. He knew he had to react somehow so the doctor would lower his gun.

"I am right here," stated Patrick.

The second Dr. Muller saw Patrick show himself from around the corner of the cabin, he pointed his gun toward him and told him not to get any closer.

"Where is my sister? Is she inside the cabin?" asked Patrick as he kept going closer to the doctor.

"I told you not to get any closer!" responded the doctor as he stretched his arm with his pistol now aimed toward Patrick's head.

The tension between Patrick and Dr. Muller only escalated, and the driver began to fear for his life.

"What's going on, Patrick?" asked the driver.

"Don't you worry about what is going on! But who the fuck are you anyway? You still didn't answer!" answered the doctor as he switched his aim to the driver's head. This gave Patrick the opportunity to try to disarm the doctor.

Yet, out of the corner of his eye, the doctor saw Patrick rushing toward him, so he quickly turned toward Patrick and shot him.

Patrick fell to the ground, and nothing could be worse for Octavian than to watch his father get shot right in front of his eyes. Reacting instantly, Octavian charged at Dr Muller like a young bull seeing red. He jumped onto the doctor's back, causing both of them to fall to the ground, just as his dad had. As the doctor tried to protect himself from falling onto his face, his pistol flew through the air, landing right next to Patrick, who was trying to get up with his right hand pressed over his bleeding left shoulder, reaching for the fallen weapon.

"Get the fuck off my back!" exclaimed the doctor as he threw Octavian onto the ground and reached out for the gun.

The taxi driver, without hesitation, hauled off and kicked the doctor solidly in the head with the full force of his boot, knocking him out cold before he could grab the pistol. This gave Patrick the chance to get the gun first.

"Shoot that piece of shit!" shouted the driver once Patrick had the pistol.

"I don't think he's breathing any longer!" said Patrick as he leaned over the doctor, who had a bloody nose and a split open eye from the kick to his head.

Then, as he turned to his son, he asked him if he was hurt.

"No, I'm all right, Dad. But you just got shot!" answered Octavian as he clenched his arms around his father, helping him stand up.

"I'm all right, too. You were very brave jumping on the doctor like that. But now, please go hide behind those trees and wait for me there. I need to find out if Maria is in this cabin," continued Patrick as he unclenched his son's arms from around him.

In the meantime, the driver cautiously walked by the cabin window, and because he didn't see anybody inside, he began to relax a little bit.

"Patrick! I believe nobody else is in the cabin. What's going on in here?"

"I don't have a clue, but I am about to find out. I saw the doctor coming out of a secret door, and I need to find out if my sister is in there," responded Patrick.

"I'll go with you," said the taxi driver.

The driver followed Patrick into the cabin and was astonished at how effectively the floral wallpaper concealed the secret door. Patrick had opened it by pushing on a flower petal in the wallpaper, just as he had seen the doctor do.

"Now, this is very bizarre," whispered the taxi driver as they looked at the steep flight of stairs below them, which were lit up by lights on the walls.

They couldn't hear anything in the basement, and from the top of the stairs, they couldn't see anything but a really bright light.

"Please wait here in case you hear anything so you can warn me immediately," whispered Patrick before he descended the stairs cautiously with the pistol.

Patrick knew that when he was shot outside of the cabin, someone could have heard that from the basement, and perhaps they were waiting silently for someone to appear. Thus, the quiet basement did not put Patrick at ease; on the contrary, it only focused his attention more acutely with every step. Once he was at the bottom of the stairs, he nervously stuck his head out from behind the wall to see what was there.

The basement looked like a medical lab, and to his surprise, he saw a human body flat down on its stomach on the floor next to a bed inside one of the two odd cages built across the room in what seemed like some sort of thick clear acrylic. Moreover, the walls of the cages were built from the floor all the way up to the ceiling, and what was even stranger was that the cages were built next to each other and separated with the same thick clear acrylic. It seemed like the person who built these cages wanted to make sure there wouldn't be any privacy.

Patrick couldn't tell if the body in the cage was a man or a woman, dead or alive. As soon he got by the cages with his pistol drawn, he saw that it was a man wearing a bloody hospital gown similar to Maria's. The man appeared to be unconscious. Fresh wounds on his knuckles and blood on the inside of the acrylic door suggested that the man had been trying to break out. An electric cattle prod hanging on a hook outside the door could explain why the man was passed out.

The cage door was locked. And Patrick couldn't find any keys nearby. Since Maria was not in the basement, he faced a decision: leave right away to try and catch the ambulance that might have his sister or stay to help the wounded man escape from the cage.

"Patrick!" the driver whispered loudly from the top of the stairs.

Because Patrick was already on high alert, he thought the taxi driver was trying to warn him, so he quietly walked back to the staircase and carefully looked up the stairs.

"Is everything all right?" he asked.

"Yes, but I don't have a good feeling about this place. We should go if your sister is not down there," said the driver.

"My sister is not here, but there's a man trapped in the basement wearing a hospital gown similar to the one my sister is in. Help me get him out, and we'll leave right after. We can't leave him here," said Patrick.

The taxi driver went down the stairs, and he couldn't believe what he saw.

"What the fuck is this place? We should leave right away!"

"Help me look for the keys that might open that lock, or we might have to break the door," shouted Patrick.

Meanwhile, Octavian was still waiting in the dark forest behind the first row of trees, just as his father had instructed. He kept a watchful eye on Dr. Muller's motionless body. However, it was extremely difficult to just stand there and wait, knowing that his father was inside the cabin, and the silence of the forest only made him anxious.

When a car approached with its bright lights piercing through the forest shadows, Octavian wanted to warn his father. However, the lights would have shined on him before he could reach the cabin. Unsure of who was in the car, he stayed hidden behind the tree, waiting to decide his next move.

Surprisingly, it was the male nurse driving the ambulance. As soon as he stopped and saw Dr. Muller's body on the ground, covered in blood, he reached into the waistband of his pants and pulled a pistol out. He checked for a pulse, and after he realized the doctor was still alive, he gently pulled him to the side of the cabin as he kept his eyes on the open door of the cabin.

"Dr. Muller! What happened?" he asked the doctor as he softly shook his body, hoping for an answer.

Receiving no response, the male nurse stood up, aimed his pistol at the cabin, and quietly walked inside, noticing the secret door was open. As soon as the nurse entered the cabin, Octavian approached the ambulance to see if his aunt was inside. He found Maria strapped to a stretcher, looking as though she was coming out of sedation.

"I can't find any keys!" shouted the taxi driver to Patrick.

The second the nurse heard voices in the basement, he tightened his grip around the pistol, and quietly, with his finger on the trigger, he began to descend the stairs.

"I'll check Dr. Muller's pockets. Perhaps he might have the keys. And check on my son as well. In the meantime, look for any steel bars," said Patrick as he walked toward the staircase.

The male nurse heard Patrick's voice and immediately stopped, waiting for him. He took a deep breath and started counting, "Three, two, one," anticipating Patrick's shadow to appear on the stairs, illuminated by the light from the secret room. Just before Patrick came into view, someone pushed the nurse from behind, causing him to lose his balance and fall down the stairs. Luckily, when the nurse fired his pistol, the bullet went into the ceiling.

This gave Patrick a chance to grab his own pistol and shoot the nurse two times in the head.

"Dad, are you all right?" shouted Octavian from the top of the stairs.

"I'm all right, son. Did you push him down the stairs?" asked the father.

"Yes. He came back with the ambulance, and Aunt Maria is in it. What should I do?" asked Octavian.

"Wait, I'm coming up," responded Patrick.

Patrick looked down at the nurse's body, and he noticed some keys hanging from the loop of his waistband.

"I found keys that might unlock the cage!" shouted Patrick to the driver, who was watching the man in the cage trying to stand up.

Patrick threw the keys to the taxi driver.

"There you go. Let's find out if they'll open the door!" shouted Patrick as he walked toward the cage.

"This is it!" yelled the driver on his second attempt to open the lock.

The man from inside the cage looked like he was struggling to pick himself up.

"Who are you?" asked Patrick in German.

But the man's answer didn't match Patrick's question.

"If you do anything to her, I will kill you all!" he said in German with wrath in his voice as he grabbed the metal frame of the bed to pull himself up off of the floor.

The man's ankle was chained to the bed. Patrick didn't know the man's story or what to expect from him, so he approached him cautiously with his finger on the trigger.

"We're here to help! But what is your connection to Dr. Muller?" asked Patrick, but hearing Dr. Muller's name only enraged the caged man.

"I'll kill that motherfucker!" he shouted as he lifted his head higher and looked into Patrick's eyes.

The second Patrick looked into the man's eyes, he instantly lowered his pistol and shouted in Romanian, "This can't be possible!" The caged man fell silent, and the look of rage in his eyes began to fade.

"Maximus, is that you?" Patrick asked in Romanian, still in disbelief that the man in the cage could be his brother-in-law. The caged man said nothing.

"My brother, is that really you?" Patrick continued asking. As he got closer, he saw the caged man's eyes fill with tears.

"You can't be real," Maximus cried, placing his hand on Patrick's shoulder.

"Let's get you out of here," said Patrick as he took the keys from the taxi driver so he could unlock the chain that was holding Maximus prisoner in the cage.

"Where's Maria? Please tell me she's all right. Dr. Muller brought her here unconscious, and he said that he would kill both of us," said Maximus while he watched Patrick try to open the lock.

Luckily, one of the keys opened the lock, and Maximus was freed from the thick metal shackle that was on his ankle.

"Maria is all right. My son just told me that she is outside in the ambulance and—"

Before Patrick could finish his sentence, Octavian shouted from the top of the stairs, "Dad, Dr. Muller is up, and he's walking toward the ambulance."

Maximus didn't wait to hear anything else; he ran up the stairs like his ankle had never been shackled to a bed frame and as if he weren't injured. Patrick followed closely behind, pistol ready. Octavian stepped aside as Maximus rushed out of the cabin.

It was clear that Dr. Muller was badly injured, as he was limping toward the ambulance. Despite his condition, he managed to reach the driver's side door. Just then, Maximus grabbed the doctor by his shirt and violently pulled him to the ground.

"Where do you think you're going, you piece of shit!" yelled Maximus as he watched the doctor try to crawl away.

Maximus walked over to Dr. Muller and mercilessly stomped on his back, then kicked him in the ribs until the doctor rolled onto his back. Maximus then jumped on top of him and began pounding his face relentlessly. Patrick, Octavian, and the taxi driver watched, feeling there was no reason to intervene.

Suddenly, Maria's voice was heard from inside the ambulance. She was coming out of sedation, confused to find herself tied to a stretcher and alone in the back of the ambulance. She began calling for anyone who could hear her.

Hearing Maria's voice, Maximus stopped his assault on the doctor before it turned fatal and rushed to the back of the ambulance. As he opened the back doors, the interior lights came on, and Maria could just barely lift her head to see the figure of a man who looked like Maximus. Thinking it was another dream, she closed her eyes, laid her head back on the pillow, and waited to wake up.

This time, however, she felt a gentle caress on her cheek and heard Maximus calling her name. She opened her eyes to find him standing right next to her. Looking into her eyes, Maximus wrapped his arms around Maria in a long-awaited embrace and said, "I never lost hope that I could somehow hold you in my arms again."

Maria reached out and touched Maximus's face, astonished that his image was not vanishing like it had in her previous dreams. Her hand stayed on his cheek, and she whispered to herself, "Please, God, keep me stranded in this dream forever," as she gazed deeply into Maximus's eyes.

Patrick and Octavian walked to the back of the ambulance to check on Maria. Meanwhile, the cab driver dragged Dr. Muller, who was still unconscious but breathing, into the cabin and chained him in one of the cages from the basement.

"Maria, you have finally found Maximus!" Patrick exclaimed with a big smile as he jumped into the back of the ambulance.

Maria looked at Patrick and Octavian, still confused. She felt wide awake, yet Maximus was still there, holding her. With tears in her eyes, she asked, "Do you see him, too?"

"Yes, I do. He is right there in your arms," Patrick confirmed, pointing at Maximus.

Dr. Muller, also known as Lieutenant Muller during the Second World War, was a lieutenant deeply involved in the massacre in Odessa. On the night Maximus opened the doors to help Jews escape, Lieutenant Muller and his squad were tasked with catching everyone who escaped. While hundreds of Jews escaped, several dozen were caught. Among them, Maximus was Muller's biggest catch. Although Muller initially wanted to kill Maximus on the spot for what he did, he found greater satisfaction in making Maximus's life a living hell. That same night, Lieutenant Muller made it seem like Maximus disappeared from the face of the earth by sending him with one of his German soldiers to a cabin outside of Munich.

After the war, Dr. Muller and the soldier continued to conduct horrific experiments on abducted Jews, including children, with Maximus forced to watch. This cruel secret remained unknown to everyone, including Dr. Klaus.

In the end, Dr. Muller, with his hands and feet tied, bled to death in his own cabin from the beating he received from Maximus. He met the fate he deserved: dead and not mourned.

THE END

Another Joshua Tree Publishing Book by Bogdan Sopterean

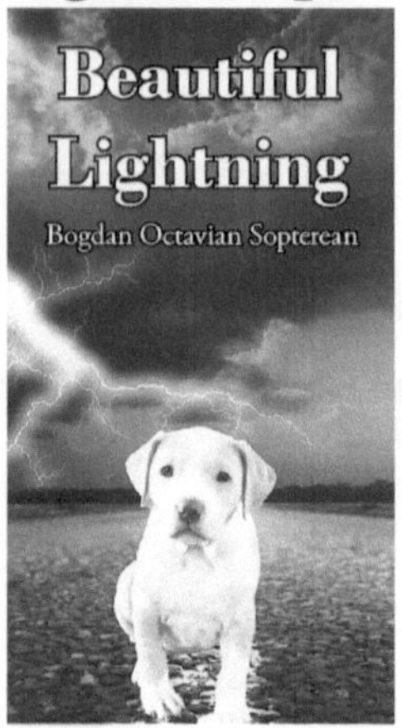

Beautiful Lightning is not just another heartwarming tale of the magical connection between man's best friend and people. It is a unique true story where the author gratefully puts together the pieces of a puzzle he gathers throughout his journey that he and his family took with their rescued dog Bella whose breed faces a lot of prejudice and presented challenges for his entire family from the first day they adopted her.

However, Bella became part of the family, too. Because their bond was so strong, they decided to do whatever it took to make things work out. Although, when things finally started heading in the right direction, the family received extremely bad news that sent them into a tail spin and the events that happened next left them devastated.

As soon as the author gets the most important puzzle piece and begins connecting the pieces together, he realizes that all of them have been left behind for him intentionally and with a purpose.

About the Author

Bogdan Sopterean was born on October 1, 1980, in Cluj-Napoca, Romania, which is located in the beautiful region of Transylvania—yes, the region where Dracula was born. When he began middle school, he started to practice martial arts, which helped him to become more focused in school and helped him learn to believe in himself. By age seventeen, he was a black belt and was part of the Romanian National Karate Team.

He graduated from Nicolae Balcescu High School, where Spanish, English and Romanian were his major courses. Because sports were already a big part of his life, he graduated from Babes-Bolyai University in Cluj-Napoca, Romania, with a Bachelor's Degree in Physical Education and Sports.

In 2002, Bogdan decided to move to America, known as the land of opportunity, where one could achieve anything they put their mind to, no matter who they are, and ever since, he looked for his calling.

His true passion for writing came at a difficult time in his life, but at that moment, he discovered that writing books is his calling and that he will never stop writing.

Presently, Bogdan and his lovely wife Natali live in Lake Zurich, Illinois with their beautiful fifteen-year-old daughter Sydney and their dog Grace.

www.ingramcontent.com/pod-product-compliance
Lightning Source LLC
Chambersburg PA
CBHW031443200726

48289CB00007BB/2182